PURE POISON!

The boat lurched to a stop, and Frank and Nancy had to grab the sides to keep from losing their balance.

"Uh-oh," Nancy said, peering over the side of the *Blue Liner*. "Looks like we hit some of those shallows Mama Gayle warned us about."

While Nancy angled the motor up out of the water, Frank reached for the pole from the bottom of the boat. As he pulled it from beneath the tarp, a flickering movement caught his attention. A striped brown snake slithered from beneath the tarp. When Frank saw its splotchy brown coloring and the pitted indentations next to its eyes, he gasped.

"Nancy, watch out!" Frank shouted. "There's a water moccasin heading right for your feet!"

Nancy Drew & Hardy Boys SuperMysteries

Available from ARCHWAY Paperbacks

A NANCY AND HARDY DREW BOYS SUPER MYSTERY™

NIGHTMARE IN NEW ORLEANS

Carolyn Keene

AN ARCHWAY PAPERBACK
Published by POCKET BOOKS
New York London Toronto Sydney Tokyo Singapore

AN ARCHWAY PAPERBACK *Original*

An Archway Paperback published by
POCKET BOOKS, a division of Simon & Schuster Inc.
1230 Avenue of the Americas, New York, NY 10020

ISBN: 0-671-53749-0

First Archway Paperback printing March 1997

10 9 8 7 6 5 4 3 2 1

Cover art by Franco Accornero

Printed in the U.S.A.

IL 6+

NIGHTMARE IN NEW ORLEANS

Chapter

One

"NEW ORLEANS—what an amazing place," Joe Hardy said to his brother, Frank.

"I know what you mean," Frank agreed. He stuck his hands in his jeans pockets and looked out from the wharf where he and Joe stood. Before them, the muddy waters of the Mississippi River flowed lazily past. High-rise hotels and the International Trade Mart towered over the stores and tourist attractions of the renovated waterfront. Beyond it, Frank caught a glimpse of colonial houses, ornate wrought-iron railings and balconies, and tropical flowers and trees he couldn't begin to name. Farther upriver were the rotting back sides of some abandoned warehouses and docks. "It feels like a mix of everything that's exotic, exciting, and decadent," he declared.

"Not to mention gorgeous," Joe added, glancing

appreciatively at a tall blond who was just passing by. "I think I'm going to like it here."

Frank had to roll his eyes at that one. It figured that the biggest flirt in North America would be his own brother. "We're here on a case, remember?" he reminded Joe. "Finding half a million dollars?"

"And the thief who stole it from Hugh Gatlin's riverboat casino," Joe added. The playful gleam disappeared from his blue eyes and was replaced by a look of steely determination. He nodded toward a low glass-and-concrete building next to the wharf. A sign over the entrance read *Delta Princess* Casino Tours. "We might as well head to Gatlin's office and get all the details."

Hugh Gatlin was the owner of the *Delta Princess* riverboat casino. He'd known the Hardys' father, Fenton, since their college days. Late the night before, Mr. Gatlin had called with disturbing news: Someone had broken into the riverboat's safe and made off with over half a million dollars. The police were on the case, but Gatlin had decided to call in Frank and Joe, too, hoping that would increase the odds of finding the thief quickly. The brothers had flown to New Orleans on the earliest flight that morning. They had dropped off their bags with the housekeeper at Mr. Gatlin's house, quickly eaten sandwiches she had prepared for them, then made their way to his office immediately.

"Hi," Frank said to the receptionist as he and Joe stepped into the Casino Tours office. She was standing behind a long, sleek counter covered with

schedules and publicity brochures. Framed photographs of New Orleans and the *Delta Princess,* an old-fashioned steam-powered paddleboat, decorated the walls. When Frank introduced himself and Joe, the receptionist smiled and nodded.

"Mr. Gatlin is expecting you," she said in a lilting drawl. "Why don't y'all come on back with me?"

She led Frank and Joe behind the counter and through a door to a network of offices, then up a flight of stairs, where she stopped outside a door. "You can go on in," she said.

"Pretty impressive," Joe said softly to Frank as they entered the large office. There was a mix of antique furniture and high-tech computer and audiovisual equipment. Huge windows wrapped around the office on three sides, providing a breathtaking view of the waterfront.

"Frank! Joe!" The man who got up from behind the mahogany desk was portly and amiable, with short dark hair and astute gray eyes. His linen suit jacket was draped around the back of his chair, and his sleeves were rolled up. A wide smile spread across his face as he came over and gave each of the Hardys a firm handshake. "Thanks for coming on such short notice."

"No problem," Joe said. "Frank and I can start right in as soon as you brief us about what happened."

Mr. Gatlin sat back down behind his desk and gestured for the Hardys to take the two chairs in front of it. "I guess I'd better start at the beginning," he said, rubbing his chin. "The *Princess* goes

out on half a dozen cruises a day, docking for the night around eleven-thirty. An armored truck meets the boat to pick up the money. There's a safe on board, of course, as well as security cameras, an alarm, guards—" He took a deep breath and let it out slowly. "I thought it was a foolproof system."

"Do you have any reason to believe it was an inside job?" Joe asked.

"No," Mr. Gatlin replied. "I trust my employees. Most everyone's been with me for years. I feel I know the people who work for me pretty well."

"How exactly did the thief strike?" Frank asked.

"He knocked out the guard from behind," Mr. Gatlin explained. "Then he sprayed paint over the security camera's lens, blew open the safe with plastic explosives, and was gone before anyone knew what had happened. With all the commotion of people leaving the riverboat, no one heard or saw him. The only person who noticed the explosion was J. J."

"J. J.?" Joe echoed, sitting forward in his chair. "Who's he?"

"J. J. Johnson. He plays the trumpet in the brass band that provides entertainment during our evening cruise," Mr. Gatlin answered. He grimaced before adding, "Unfortunately, J. J. didn't actually *see* anything, since he's blind. He was on the deck, not far from the office where the safe is. He heard the explosion and then heard the thief run past and climb down the paddle wheel. Whoever it was got away on a motorboat."

That doesn't give us much to go on, Frank thought, but at least it's something. "We'd like to

talk to J. J.," he told Mr. Gatlin. "And to the guard who was knocked out. Maybe one of them remembers something that could help us."

"The police have already spoken to both J. J. Johnson and Mike Keyes—he's the guard," Mr. Gatlin said. "I've let J. J. know that he'll be hearing from y'all. And Mike said he'd stop by to talk to you this afternoon." He glanced out the window, then flashed a quick smile. "As a matter of fact, he's pulling up right now."

Frank saw a beat-up red convertible pulling into a parking spot in the lot next to the Casino Tours office. A tall man wearing mirrored sunglasses, black jeans, and cowboy boots hopped out. Even from the office, it was impossible to miss the way his biceps bulged beneath his black T-shirt. When he appeared in Hugh Gatlin's office a few minutes later, the guy seemed to fill up the entire doorway.

"Hey, Mr. G.," Mike said in an easy drawl. A few long strides carried him across the room to Hugh Gatlin's desk. As he pushed his sunglasses up on top of his head, Frank saw that Mike was only a few years older than he and Joe—maybe in his early twenties. Even though he had a formidable build, his windblown brown hair and freckled face gave him a boyish look.

When Gatlin introduced Frank and Joe, Mike stood beside Mr. Gatlin's desk and carefully looked the Hardys over. "So, y'all think you can do a better job of finding Mr. G.'s money than the New Orleans Police Department?" he asked.

Frank could see Joe bristle at the challenging tone of Mike's voice. He leaned forward in his

chair, his eyes flashing with anger. "For your information," Joe said, "Frank and I have solved hundreds of—"

"We're just trying to help. It's not a competition," Frank cut in, giving Joe a warning look. Getting into an argument with a guy who was built like a Mack truck didn't seem like the greatest idea—especially since they needed Mike's help.

"Mike takes his job very, very seriously," Mr. Gatlin said to Frank and Joe. "When something goes wrong, he gets upset about it."

Mr. Gatlin turned to the guard. "These boys are not trying to muscle in on your territory, Mike. Just tell Frank and Joe everything you remember, and maybe we can solve this thing even faster."

"There's not a whole lot to tell," Mike said, shrugging. "Let's see . . ." He went over to the window, leaned against the sill, and crossed his arms over his massive chest. "It happened after the *Princess* docked for the night. I was making a final round of the boat, and then I went into the office where the safe is."

"Was the room locked?" Joe asked.

Mike nodded. "It was locked and the alarm was on," he answered. His eyes held a mocking glint.

He obviously wasn't taking them seriously, Joe thought, but at least he was cooperating.

"After I disabled the alarm, unlocked the door, and went inside, someone came up from behind and hit me," Mike continued. He reached up, grimacing as he touched a spot on the back of his head. "When I came to, the safe was busted open, and whoever had knocked me out was gone."

"With half a million dollars of *my* money!" Hugh Gatlin added. "The police found small bits of plastic explosive near the safe, and a metal pipe in the hall where Mike was knocked out. They dusted the whole area for prints, but everything was clean."

"They found the pipe in the hall? I thought you said you were *inside* the room where the safe is when the thief hit you," Joe said, turning to Mike.

Hugh Gatlin shook his head and frowned. "He's right, Mike. I was right there when you spoke to the police. I clearly remember you telling them you were struck from behind in the hall."

Mike hesitated a moment before he answered. "I guess you could say I was right *at* the doorway. Not exactly in *or* out."

Frank couldn't be sure, but he had the feeling Mike wasn't telling them the whole story. Judging by the doubtful look on Joe's face, Frank thought his brother felt the same way. "You didn't see anyone else, either before you were knocked out or after you came to?" Frank asked.

Mike shook his head. "Not till I went out on the balcony and found J. J. there," he replied.

"The safe's located on the upper level of the riverboat, above the gaming rooms, snack bar, and jazz club. The area's usually fairly deserted," Mr. Gatlin explained. "That's why no one else heard the blast."

So, except for J. J. there was no one else who could confirm or contradict Mike's story, Frank realized. As Mike crossed one ankle in front of the other, Frank noticed his cowboy boots. They were made of shiny black snakeskin and looked brand-new—and very expensive. Of course, having new boots didn't make the guy a criminal, Frank reminded himself.

"You don't have any idea at all who could have stolen the money?" he asked Mike.

Instead of answering, Mike turned to Hugh Gatlin and asked, "You didn't show them the tape?"

"Not yet." Gatlin picked up a videocassette from his desk and went over to the TV and VCR in a built-in console against one wall. "There was a man at the blackjack table last night," he said, talking over his shoulder to Frank and Joe. "He was losing big and wasn't happy about it. One of our security cameras got him on tape."

He pushed a few buttons, and seconds later the blackjack table flashed onto the screen. The camera gave a distorted, black-and-white view of half a dozen people around the table, with others watching or threading their way through the crowd behind. The atmosphere was lively and chaotic, from what Frank could tell. Then he spotted a man at the edge of the screen.

The man appeared to be extremely agitated. His dark, thick brows were knitted together. He muttered angrily at the people around him while he played. When he lost the hand and the dealer swept away his chips, he jumped up and started yelling. Then he grabbed the dealer by the shirt.

"Whoa," Joe muttered under his breath.

"The guy threatened the dealer, accused him of cheating," Mike said. "That's where I came in."

A beefy arm flashed onto the screen. Then Mike

could be seen, wearing a jacket with a badge saying Security on the lapel. He pulled the dark-haired man away from the dealer.

The next few moments were a blur of flailing arms and shouting faces. Finally, the dark-haired man reached down and grabbed a white canvas tote bag from the floor. He put the straps of the bag over one shoulder, and Frank could make out that the logo on the bag was a chef's cap with some letters emblazoned on it.

As the man stormed from the gaming room, Mr. Gatlin stopped the tape. "His name is Remy Maspero," Hugh Gatlin said. "Mike was able to find that out from some of the other people who were at the blackjack table with him. Apparently, he's about to open a new Creole restaurant here in New Orleans."

Frank nodded, mentally filing away the information. "Did you see where Maspero went after that?" he asked Mike.

"To the Dixieland Jazz Bar we have on board. I checked up on him a few times, but he was quiet," Mike said. "Once the *Princess* docked, I stopped worrying about the guy. I assumed he had left along with everyone else. But who knows? Maybe he decided to steal back the money he lost."

"And then some," Joe added. "We should talk to him, Frank."

"I'd like to talk to J. J. Johnson, too," Frank said, "and take a look at the *Delta Princess.*"

Hugh Gatlin nodded out the window at the empty wharf next to the office. "The *Princess* is upriver on a cruise now, but I'll arrange for you two to be on the evening tour. It leaves here at seven forty-five. Mike will be working, so he'll show you the area around the safe. I'm going to be busy the next few days, preparing a speech for a conference of local business leaders. My daughter, Faye, said she'd help you find your way around town and get you anything you might need."

"Great," Joe said. "Was she by any chance on the *Delta Princess* last night, too?"

"No. Faye and I were out celebrating my birthday with a late dinner when Mike beeped me and relayed the bad news," Mr. Gatlin answered. "Some birthday present, eh?"

"Mmm," Frank said distractedly. He wasn't crazy about the idea of including Mr. Gatlin's daughter in the investigation. She would probably just get in the way. "About your daughter—Joe and I can handle things fine on our own," he told Mr. Gatlin. "We're used to—"

"Hi, Daddy," a bright voice spoke up from behind Frank. "Sorry I'm late."

Turning around, Frank saw a tall young woman striding through the office doorway. She was about his age, Frank guessed, with intelligent green eyes and straight dark hair that fell halfway down her back. As she stepped lightly across the room toward Hugh, Frank couldn't help noticing the way her flowered skirt billowed around her slender legs.

"Hello, darlin'." Hugh Gatlin gave her a kiss on the cheek, then smiled proudly as he turned to Frank and Joe. "This is my daughter, Faye. Faye, meet—"

"Frank and Joe Hardy," Faye supplied. She held

out a hand, grinning. "Daddy's told me all about you. I don't know if I'll be much help to y'all, but I'm willing to give it a shot if you are."

As Frank shook her hand, he found himself staring into her eyes longer than he'd intended. "I, uh—that'd be great," he mumbled.

"Smooth, Frank," Joe said under his breath. More loudly, he added, "What was it you were just saying, Frank? Something about how we work alo—"

"It was nothing," Frank cut in.

"Good. It's settled, then," Mr. Gatlin said, with a broad smile. "I have business to attend to, so if you don't mind . . ."

"I'm sure we can find some place to talk everything over." Faye raised an eyebrow at Frank and Joe. "How about coffee and beignets at the Café du Monde? It's not far from here. It's right in the thick of the French Quarter."

Frank didn't even know what beignets were, but he found himself smiling back at Faye. "Sure," he told her. "Sounds terrific."

Joe stared across the café table at Frank and Faye Gatlin. Here I am, sitting outside at the Café du Monde with the most gorgeous girl in New Orleans, he thought. And she's flirting with my brother.

Joe took a sip of his coffee. He felt out of place, and he didn't like it. Frank wasn't usually the flirting type—that was more *his* department, Joe thought. But Joe recognized the signs—the subtle gleam of interest in his brother's eyes, the way he listened so attentively to everything Faye said. It was enough to make Joe choke on the square powdery doughnuts Faye called beignets.

"If you'd like, we can talk to J. J. Johnson before tonight's tour on the *Princess,*" Faye was saying, her green eyes fixed on Frank. "According to Daddy, he spends a lot of time at Dupre's, a jazz club over on Bourbon Street."

"The sooner the better," Joe said. He was itching to get started on the case, but neither Faye nor Frank even seemed to hear him.

"I'd like to learn more about Mike Keyes, too," Frank said. He inched his chair slightly closer to Faye's, then took a sip of his coffee. "There's something about the guy I don't trust."

"Like the way he hedged about where he was when he was knocked out?" Joe put in.

This time Joe noted that Frank actually looked at him for half a second and nodded before turning back to Faye. "What do you know about Mike?" he asked her.

"I've known Mike just about all my life. He was a few years ahead of me in school, but our families have always been friendly. He and my dad play golf together. I don't socialize with him, though. He travels in a much faster crowd than I do." Faye ran a hand through her long dark hair and stared out from beneath the café's striped awning at the tourists bustling past. "Mike likes to have a good time," she continued, "tearing around in his convertible, staying up till all hours playing poker . . ."

She seemed perceptive, Joe had to admit. And

smart. She reminded him of someone, but he couldn't put his finger on who it was.

"I'm busy with college and a job at Michaud's Department Store at the mall, so I don't see Mike much anymore," Faye went on. "Still, I'd say he's harmless. Daddy wouldn't keep him on at the *Delta Princess* if he thought otherwise." Suddenly she looked worried as she turned back to Frank. "You don't think he had anything to do with last night's theft, do you? Our families have known each other forever."

"It's a possibility we should keep in mind, that's all," Joe said. "We can't afford to—"

"Frank and Joe Hardy!" a familiar voice called from the street. "Is it really you?"

Joe whipped his head around, and his mouth dropped open in surprise. "Hey! It's Nancy and Bess!"

Nancy Drew, Bess Marvin, and a blond-haired young woman Joe didn't recognize were standing in front of a redbrick building whose double porches were lined with decorative ironwork, fancy pillars, and mossy hanging plants. The girls waved as they crossed Decatur Street in front of Jackson Square and headed toward the Café du Monde.

"I don't believe it!" Frank cried as he and Joe jumped up to give Nancy and Bess hugs.

Nancy grinned, her blue eyes flitting back and forth between Frank and Joe. "What a great surprise!"

"I'll say," Bess chimed in. "What brings you two to New Orleans?"

"My father," Faye Gatlin spoke up. "Someone

13

decided to help themselves to half a million dollars from my daddy's riverboat casino." Faye's face lit up as she smiled at Frank, who was dragging three chairs over from a nearby table. "Frank and Joe are helping to get it back."

"We heard about that on the news this morning," Nancy said. Joe noticed the curious once-over she gave Faye as she sat down on Frank's other side. Obviously, she had noticed the chemistry between Faye and Frank, too.

"Faye Gatlin, meet Nancy Drew and Bess Marvin," Frank said. "They've teamed up with Joe and me more than a few times in the past."

As Joe looked back and forth between Nancy and Faye, he realized who it was that Faye reminded him of: Nancy! They were both smart, pretty, and quick-witted. Although Frank and Nancy had never acted on it, Joe knew there was an attraction between the two. Hmm, he thought, this could get interesting. . . .

"This is our friend Shelley. She moved here from River Heights back in high school, and now she's a business major in college here." Bess's voice broke into Joe's thoughts. She grinned at the blond-haired young woman sitting next to her. "She has a break from school, and she promised Nan and me a week of totally excessive eating and partying, so naturally we flew here right away."

"Doing everything to excess is what New Orleans is all about, after all," Shelley said with a laugh. She was petite, with short blond hair, broad cheeks, and big brown eyes that shimmered with merriment.

"There's a lot to celebrate," Nancy put in. "How often does one of our friends elope with a dashing Creole chef who's about to open his own restaurant?"

Frank blinked at Shelley. "Your husband's opening a Creole restaurant?" he asked, frowning.

Joe knew exactly what his brother was thinking. Remy Maspero, the guy they'd seen threatening the blackjack dealer on the *Delta Princess* security tape, was starting up a Creole restaurant, too.

"It opens tonight," Shelley said, with an excited nod. "It's a little scary. Being a restaurateur is a competitive business in New Orleans, and Remy's sunk all his money into the place. But I know it's going to be a success."

"Remy, huh?" Joe echoed.

Suddenly he had a sinking feeling in the pit of his stomach. Before he could even look at Frank, Shelley smiled and waved at someone passing by. "Remy—over here!" she called.

Joe took one look at the guy—and gulped. There was no mistaking his thick black brows or the serious, intense expression on his handsome face.

Shelley's husband was their biggest suspect in the theft from the *Delta Princess*!

Chapter

Two

NANCY'S GAZE flew quickly back and forth between Frank and Joe. Her sleuth's instincts had kicked in as soon as they'd begun asking about Shelley's husband. She didn't miss the sober expressions that came over both Hardys' faces or the glances they exchanged with Faye as Remy approached their table. Nancy wasn't sure how, but she was willing to bet Remy was involved in their case.

"What's going on, Frank?" she whispered, leaning close to him while Remy gave Shelley a kiss.

"Remy lost a bundle on the *Delta Princess* last night," Frank whispered back, his eyes still on Remy. "Hugh Gatlin thinks he could be the person who robbed the riverboat."

"Oh, no," Nancy said, under her breath. "But how could that be? Remy's been completely caught

16

up in getting ready to open his restaurant. He didn't even have dinner with us last night because there were still so many details to take care of before tonight's opening."

At least, that was what Remy had *said* when Nancy and Bess stopped by the restaurant with Shelley after their arrival the previous afternoon. He hadn't mentioned a word about plans to go on a riverboat casino. Now that Nancy thought about it, she realized Remy had seemed on edge ever since she and Bess had met him. There were dark circles under his eyes, and he seemed to be frowning constantly. She'd assumed he was just stressed out from preparing to open the restaurant. Now she had to ask herself if there was something more going on.

"This is Remy," Shelley said, turning to Frank and Joe. "Part owner and head chef of the Royal Creole, a new restaurant that'll soon be the talk of New Orleans." Her brown eyes shone with pride as she looked up into Remy's face. "Frank and Joe are friends of Nancy and Bess. They're trying to find out who stole that money from the riverboat casino."

Uh-oh, thought Nancy. She caught the worried glances that ricocheted between Frank, Joe, and Faye. They obviously weren't happy to have one of their suspects tipped off about the investigation. And with good reason. In a flash, Remy's face filled with rage.

"So, you're here to make my life miserable, too!" he snapped. "Just like the police."

"Police?" Shelley echoed, looking confused. "Why would they be interested in *you*, Remy?"

"Remy was on the *Delta Princess* last night," Joe said. "He was playing hard—and losing."

Shelley's mouth fell open, and she turned to Remy in shock. "Gambling? You never said anything about—"

"I didn't want you to worry," Remy cut in, raking a hand impatiently through his thick dark hair. "Look, I just told everything I know to the police, and now I'm late getting to the restaurant to make the final preparations for the opening." He turned to Frank and Joe, his eyes flashing with annoyance. "The last thing I need is to field accusations from total strangers!"

"We're just trying to find out what happened," Frank put in quickly.

"Fine," Remy snapped. "Just leave me out of it!"

He turned and started to walk away, but Shelley grabbed his arm. "Wait!" She glanced nervously from Remy to Frank, Joe, and Faye. "Frank and Joe aren't accusing you, Remy. These people are friends. We all know you didn't take that money."

At least, we *hope* you didn't, Nancy amended silently. She knew it would break Shelley's heart if her husband was involved in the theft. She wondered how much Shelley knew about her new husband and made a mental note to ask her more about him.

"Frank and Joe can help prove you're innocent," Shelley went on. Looking at Remy with beseeching eyes, she suggested, "Why don't we invite them to join us this afternoon?"

"Remy's preparing a spread of all his Creole specialties for his friends and his financial backer," Bess explained to Frank, Joe, and Faye. "It'll be at five-thirty, but we're getting there an hour early. It's kind of like a christening just before the restaurant opens to the public for dinner tonight."

Remy looked dubiously at the Hardys and Faye, then gave a curt nod and said, "Fine."

It wasn't the most heartfelt invitation, but Joe smiled right away and said, "We'd love to come. We're not about to pass up the chance to sample the best Creole cooking in New Orleans, after all."

Or the opportunity to check out Remy, Nancy guessed.

As Shelley wrote down the address, Faye leaned over, tapped Frank's forearm, and grinned. "It'll be the perfect chance to show you Yankees some fine New Orleans hospitality."

Nancy noticed the special gleam in Frank's eyes as he looked at Faye. It was exactly the way he used to look at *her* sometimes. Of course, she and Frank both had separate lives, Nancy firmly reminded herself. And separate romances. They were friends, and that was that. If Frank was attracted to someone else, it was none of her business.

Right?

"Talk about a touchy situation," Frank said a half hour later as he, Joe, and Faye walked down Bourbon Street. "Investigating a guy who's married to Nancy and Bess's friend could be awkward."

"Mmm," said Joe. "But we can't let that influence us. So far, he's still our top suspect."

19

"We may have a chance to find out more about him tonight," Faye said. "But for now, let's see if J. J. Johnson is at Dupre's."

Joe looked up and down Bourbon Street, keeping an eye out for Dupre's jazz club. The atmosphere here was more gritty and raucous than at Jackson Square. Along the street, neon signs announced jazz clubs and eateries. The smells of beer and cigarettes wafted out of open doorways, hanging on the warm, moist air.

Faye stopped on the sidewalk and looked up at a slightly run-down three-story building. Cast-iron columns supported a narrow balcony with a rusted decorative railing on the second floor. The club's neon sign was off, but the front door was propped open. Joe heard a trumpet blaring from inside.

"This is the place," Faye announced, walking up to the front door. "Daddy used to be business partners with Paul Dupre, the owner, but I haven't been here for a few years." She stepped inside, calling "Hello?"

Frank and Joe stepped in behind her. Joe glanced at the round tables ringing the dance floor, the scarred wooden bar along the sidewall, and the ceiling fans hanging from the stamped-tin ceiling. One of the fans wasn't working, and the walls looked as if they could use a new coat of paint, but Joe liked the slightly seedy atmosphere.

The place was empty except for two people onstage, at the far end of the club. A man with brown skin, graying black hair, and sunglasses sat on a folding chair, playing the trumpet. Next to him stood a curly-haired young woman wearing a white T-shirt and jeans that hugged her curves. She was singing a blues song and tapping out the rhythm with her foot. When she saw Frank, Joe, and Faye, she broke off.

"We're closed," she called out. "Sorry, but you'll have to come back later."

"Danielle, it's Faye Gatlin. I've brought two friends with me. They'd like to speak with J. J. about last night's robbery."

The trumpet player had stopped playing. "Y'all must be the ones Mr. Gatlin told me to expect. Come on in."

"Frank and Joe Hardy," Joe supplied.

As Joe jogged across the club to the stage, he noticed the red-tipped white cane leaning against the older man's chair. J. J. Johnson held out his hand to Joe as he approached. "Nice to meet you, son."

He shifted slightly in his chair, then said, "Hello, Faye. I sure am sorry about the robbery. I guess you'll be wanting to hear about last night."

"Not again," the singer muttered. "Haven't you already been over what happened with the police?"

Joe looked at her in surprise. The girl's brown eyes flashed with annoyance. Still, he couldn't help noticing how striking she was, with high cheekbones, and mahogany-colored curls that fell around her face.

"We won't take long," Joe said, giving her a wide smile. "Sorry to bother you, miss . . ."

"Dupre. Danielle Dupre," the young woman

said curtly. "My uncle owns the club. We live upstairs."

"Music is in Danielle's blood," J. J. added fondly. "Whenever she's not singing here, she sings with the brass band on the *Delta Princess*. She was there with us last night, as a matter of fact."

"Good. Maybe you can help us out, too," Faye said. "Anything you can remember—"

Danielle gave Faye a look of disdain. "I'm a singer, not a spy," she said. "The only thing I pay attention to on the riverboat is the music. You should know that, Faye." With that, she turned away and began flipping through a songbook on the nearby piano.

Maybe she *is* gorgeous, thought Joe, but she's not the most helpful person I've ever met. Then again, J. J. was the person they'd come to talk to, not Danielle. "Looks like it's up to you, Mr. Johnson," Joe said. "Can you tell us what happened?"

"Please call me J. J." He tapped his trumpet thoughtfully for a few moments, then said, "The rest of the band and I usually linger on the *Princess* for a while after she comes in for the night. We have to pack up our equipment, then wait for our pay. It always takes a while, so last night I decided to wait on the upper deck, where there's a breeze."

"Near where the safe is," Frank put in.

"I didn't know it at the time, but yes," J. J. answered. "I was just standing there, when I heard a small bang coming from inside. It sounded kind of like fireworks. I was about to go check it out when someone come tearing past me like nobody's business. He was heading for the back of the boat—"

"He?" Faye broke in. "You're sure it was a man?"

J. J. nodded. "His step was heavier than a woman's. I noticed he was wearing men's cologne—some fruity, musky stuff. . . ." His voice trailed off to a chuckle. "Can't say as I'd choose to wear it myself, but it surely was distinctive."

Hmm, thought Joe. If our only clue is a *smell*, solving this case isn't going to be easy. "Do you remember anything else about the man?" he asked.

"I think he got off the boat by climbing down the paddle wheel," J. J. said. "That's what it sounded like, anyway. Right after that I heard a motorboat start up. The engine backfired a few times, but then whoever it was buzzed away upriver. I didn't figure out what had happened until a few minutes later, when Mike came out."

The trumpet player gave a sad shake of his head before going on. "The poor kid was all shaken up. He snapped at me and demanded to know what I was doing there. Not that I blame him. He was pretty upset about the money being taken."

"I see," Joe said noncommittally. After the shifty way Mike had acted in Hugh Gatlin's office, Joe still wasn't convinced that he wasn't involved.

Turning to the singer, Frank asked, "Danielle, are you sure you didn't see *anything* unusual? Maybe smell the fruity cologne J. J. just mentioned?"

For the briefest moment, Danielle's dark eyes flickered with uncertainty. Then, just as quickly, the uncertain look was gone. "How many times do

I have to tell you? I didn't see anything. I didn't hear anything," she said. "Look, J. J. and I have only a few hours to jam before we're due at the riverboat for tonight's cruise. We're working out a new arrangement. So, if you don't mind . . ."

Joe caught the questioning looks in Frank's and Faye's eyes. Obviously, they were both wondering the same thing he was: Why was Danielle so determined to get rid of them?

J. J. had said a man, not a woman, had run past him on the upper deck. Still, everything about Danielle told Joe not to trust her. He glanced furtively around the club. If he could just look around, maybe sneak into the upstairs apartment . . .

"Sorry to bother you," Joe said, giving her what he hoped looked like an apologetic smile. "But before we go, is there a bathroom I could use?"

Danielle rolled her eyes and waved toward an alcove set into the wall at the end of the bar, near the stage. "Back there," she told him.

As Joe headed toward the alcove, he shot Frank a glance over his shoulder. Frank nodded almost imperceptibly, then turned back to Danielle. "This is a great club," Frank said. "How long has your uncle owned it?"

As he stepped into the alcove, Joe tuned out his brother's voice and looked around. A hallway led past two restrooms and a kitchen. Just past the kitchen a chain was strung across the hall with an Employees Only sign hanging from it. Joe stepped over the chain and headed toward a set of French doors at the end of the hall. He didn't see any stairs to the second floor, but through the half-open doors he could see a courtyard. Perhaps there was an outside staircase, he thought.

Just then Joe saw someone streak past outside the doors. He caught a glimpse of black clothes, brown hair, and muscular arms.

Mike Keyes? he wondered. But what would he be doing here?

All Joe's senses were on red alert as he flew the rest of the way to the French doors. Even from inside, he could hear footsteps on metal stairs just outside. He pushed open the doors, then winced as they made a loud, squeaky sound.

The footsteps stopped. Joe hardly dared breathe as he stuck his head outside and looked around. The courtyard was small, with just a gravel drive running from the street to a detached carriage house behind the club. He guessed it was probably used as a garage. No stairs there.

Joe looked up and saw that he was beneath a rear balcony. Black metal steps angled up to it along the club's outside wall. He could see only the underside of the staircase, but all his instincts told him that the person was on the stairs.

Careful not to make a sound, Joe took one step into the courtyard, then another. Above him, he heard a soft clang as the person moved his foot up a step. Whoever it was had reached the top now, Joe thought, when he heard the soft rattle of a door-knob, followed by the scraping of metal. What's going on? he wondered.

He angled his head around, trying to get a better look, and—

"Whoa!" Joe cried.

A section of black wrought-iron railing was teetering over the edge of the balcony right above his head. It scraped over the edge and plummeted downward—straight toward him.

Chapter

Three

No!" JOE SHOUTED, and dived back under the balcony.

Crash!

Joe felt as if a bomb had gone off inside his head. The ground next to him exploded, and he felt hard bits of earth and gravel pelting him all over. He threw his arms over his head, but not before he felt the stinging bite of gravel against his cheek. When he finally opened his eyes, he saw that the rusted, peeling section of iron railing lay on the ground less than a hand's width from his head.

A few inches closer, and my brain would have been Jell-O, he thought. He shook his head to clear the ringing inside it, then tensed as he heard footsteps pounding down the metal stairs and onto the gravel drive. The guy was getting away!

"Stop!" Joe cried, scrambling to his feet. He tried

27

to get a look at the person, but the stairs blocked his view. By the time Joe darted out from beneath them and into the rear drive, the man had disappeared around the side of the jazz club.

"Oh, no, you don't," Joe muttered. Gritting his teeth, he took off in pursuit. He raced around the side of the jazz club in time to see the man tearing across Bourbon Street, dodging traffic. Then he angled into a narrow alleyway across from Dupre's.

Adrenaline pumped through Joe as he poured on more speed. His sneakers sent gravel flying, and within seconds he had raced the street.

I'm onto you, pal, he thought, keeping his eyes fixed on the alleyway across Bourbon Street.

"Hey! Watch where you're going!" an angry voice called.

Suddenly Joe's vision was blocked by the rearing front legs of a horse. It was practically on top of him. "Yikes!" he cried, jumping back.

The horse was pulling an open red carriage filled with tourists. As the driver struggled with the reins, trying to bring the horse under control, Joe caught a quick glimpse of half a dozen men and women clutching their seats and cameras. The carriage jerked unsteadily with the horse's skittish movements, but the driver finally got the horse under control.

"Sorry," Joe called. "Enjoy the rest of your tour!" Ignoring the stream of insults that poured from the driver's mouth, he skirted around the carriage and into the alleyway beyond.

The alley was so narrow that Joe could almost reach out and touch both sides of it. He didn't see anyone, but far ahead he spotted traffic moving on the next street. He raced through to the other end of the alley, then whipped his head around as he looked up and down Dauphine Street.

"I don't believe this," he muttered, gasping. "He's gone."

For a minute Joe just stood there, catching his breath. He was almost sure the man he'd been chasing was Mike Keyes. But what would Mike be doing sneaking around outside Dupre's?

Frustrated, Joe turned and started back toward the jazz club. Something weird is going on, he thought. And if Danielle knows anything about it, you can bet I'm going to find out.

"You're sure it was Mike?" Frank asked his brother a few minutes later. "What would he be doing here?"

As soon as Frank had heard the crash, he figured Joe had stumbled onto trouble. J. J. had stayed behind while Frank, Faye, and Danielle ran back to the rear courtyard of Dupre's to see what had happened. All they'd found was an old section of railing with dirt and gravel sprayed all around it— Joe was nowhere in sight. When he reappeared a few minutes later, walking up the gravel drive from the street, he had a bloody scratch on his cheek, and he looked anything but happy. Once Frank heard what had happened, he understood why.

"I don't know why Mike would be here, but I'm almost positive it was him," Joe answered Frank. He nodded toward the metal stairs that rose up the outside wall to the second floor. "He went up there.

And he didn't want to be seen—badly enough to try to brain me with that piece of railing."

Danielle frowned down at the decrepit railing. "Uncle Paul's been doing repairs," she said slowly. "He had a new balcony railing installed just a few days ago. I guess he didn't have time to dispose of the old pieces yet."

Joe glowered at Danielle. "Has Mike been to the club before?" he asked, his jaw tight. "I mean, if you two are friends, that could explain why he was here."

Frank knew that Joe was really wondering whether Mike and Danielle could somehow have worked together to steal the money from the *Delta Princess.*

Danielle didn't answer right away, but simply stood there with an irritated expression on her face. "Mike's been here a few times for jazz shows, but that's it," she finally said. "We've never hung out socially."

"So what *was* he doing here?" Faye asked, frowning.

Frank glanced up at the second-floor balcony. "Maybe Mike left some clue up there," he said.

"That's private up there," Danielle objected.

"If someone was up there," Frank said, "we should check it out. We can't be too safe."

Before Danielle could object further, Frank had jogged up the stairs and was looking around. All he saw were a few wicker chairs and some sections of rusted railing leaning against the wall.

As long as I'm here, he thought, it can't hurt to take a peek inside. Frank tried to look through the windows into the upstairs apartment, but the wooden shutters were closed. He tried the door, but it was locked. Disappointed, he leaned over the railing and looked down at the group. "Nothing special here," he reported.

Danielle fixed him with a fierce gaze as he came back down to the courtyard. "Thanks for checking," she said sarcastically. Then she started back toward the French doors.

As Frank, Joe, and Faye followed, Frank leaned close to Joe and whispered, "The upstairs apartment is locked up tight. We'll have to find another way to get up there and check it out."

He stopped talking as they entered the main room of the club and he saw that someone else was with J. J. and Danielle. The man looked as if he was in his forties. He had the same high cheekbones and reddish brown hair as Danielle, but he was leaner, with a wiry build and a short, almost military haircut. Danielle's uncle, Paul Dupre, Frank guessed. The man was just pulling a black ceiling fan from a large cardboard box. As he looked up, Frank noticed the tense wrinkles around his eyes and mouth.

"Uncle Paul, this is Frank and Joe Hardy," Danielle said, gesturing to the Hardys.

"Nice to meet you," Mr. Dupre said. He gave them a distracted smile, but it disappeared as soon as Faye emerged from the back hall.

"Faye Gatlin?" he asked, biting off the two words. "What are *you* doing here?"

What's going on? Frank wondered. Paul Dupre was acting as if Faye were some kind of alien creature.

"Hi, Mr. Dupre," Faye said, giving him a nervous smile. "I'm here with Frank and Joe. Daddy asked them to talk to J. J. about the money that was stolen from the riverboat last night."

Paul gave the Hardys a second look that was decidedly cooler than the first. "Oh" was all he said. Then he turned back to the ceiling fan.

"The boys had a bit of a close call just now," J. J. announced from his chair on the stage. "Joe here nearly got hit by a piece of railing."

"I think Mike Keyes dropped it on me," Joe added. "It sounded to me like he was trying to sneak into your upstairs apartment."

"Mike Keyes? That troublemaker was nosing around my club?" Paul straightened up again, shooting a worried gaze around the club. "He must have been up to no good." He stared at Faye with open suspicion. "He was probably on a mission for your father!"

Faye's mouth fell open. "What! Daddy would never—"

"Hugh Gatlin is nothing but a low-down sneak!" Paul spat out. He face shook with rage as he pointed toward the exit. "I want you three out of here!"

"Mr. Dupre," Frank began, "if we could just—"

"Now!" the club owner shouted.

Nothing was going to change Mr. Dupre's mind, Frank saw. He, Joe, and Faye had no choice but to leave. "Thanks for your help, J. J.," Frank said. "'Bye, Danielle."

The singer didn't acknowledge Frank at all. He turned and followed Joe and Faye out of the club.

"What was *that* all about?" Joe asked, once they were out on the sidewalk. "What's Mr. Dupre got against your father?"

Faye frowned as she walked slowly away from the club. "When Mr. Dupre first opened the club, about ten years ago, Daddy was his business partner," she explained. "They always got along fine."

"Until . . . ?" Frank asked.

"A few years ago Daddy decided to buy the *Delta Princess,*" Faye went on. "He needed to put just about all his assets into the riverboat, so he pulled out of the club. The trouble was, Mr. Dupre couldn't afford to buy him out, so Daddy sold his share of the club to someone else, a guy named Ellis Marsden."

"Let me guess. The partnership didn't work out?" Frank said.

Faye gave a bitter laugh. "That's the understatement of the year," she said. "The guy turned out to be a crook. He embezzled thousands of dollars from the club. By the time Mr. Dupre realized what was going on, Mr. Marsden had disappeared, and the club had serious money troubles."

Joe let out a low whistle. "Wow. Sounds like a tough break."

"Mmm. Daddy felt awful," Faye said. "He had no idea Ellis Marsden was such a cheat, but Mr. Dupre doesn't see it that way. He blamed the whole thing on Daddy. Since then, he's only barely managed to keep the place afloat. And he won't even talk to Daddy. I don't think he much likes Danielle singing on the riverboat, but he knows she needs to make money. She hardly makes anything at the club because Mr. Dupre can't afford to pay her and the musicians."

Frank shot a probing look at his brother and asked, "Are you thinking what I'm thinking?"

"Stealing half a million dollars would be a way of solving Dupre's money troubles," Joe said.

"And a way to get back at my daddy," Faye added, frowning. Her green eyes flickered back and forth between Frank and Joe. "I don't know if Mr. Dupre was on the riverboat last night, but Danielle was. I suppose he could have convinced her to help him out."

"That could explain why Danielle was less than helpful to us today," Joe said.

"And not exactly friendly," Frank added.

Faye looked at Frank and nodded in agreement. Every time she looked at him, Frank felt that her green eyes were drawing him toward her like a magnet. He shook himself, forcing himself to concentrate on the case. "Danielle and Mike will both be on tonight's cruise," he said. "We'll definitely keep an eye on them."

"Look at the balconies on that house, you guys." Bess paused on Dauphine Street, in the French Quarter, and gazed up at a three-story brick house. It had columns, curved windows, and slatted shutters. Iron grillwork decorated all three floors in a delicate design of oak leaves and acorns.

"They're gorgeous," Nancy agreed. She breathed in the perfumed scent of the ivory magnolia in front of the house, then checked her watch. "I hate to say it, but shouldn't we get back to your apartment soon, Shelley?"

They'd been on a walking tour of the French Quarter since leaving the Café du Monde. But it was already a little after three o'clock and they still had to shower and change before getting to the Royal Creole at four-thirty.

"I guess we should," Shelley agreed. "I'd like to get over to the restaurant as soon as we can. Remy could use some moral support." She frowned.

Shelley was usually so cheerful, Nancy thought, but she'd been distracted ever since learning that Remy had been gambling on the *Delta Princess* the night before. Before Remy left the café, Shelley had taken him aside to talk to him. She hadn't volunteered what Remy had said, but Nancy had a feeling Shelley was still upset about it.

"Tell me again how you and Remy met," Nancy asked as they walked.

"He enrolled in a business course I was taking," Shelley began. "One day I sat down next to him and we struck up a conversation. He told me all about wanting to open a restaurant and how he needed to get some business background. I found him charming from the very beginning, from his accent to the way he could prepare a delicious, and romantic, meal in no time flat. He offered to show me around New Orleans—you know, see the place through the eyes of a native. We had so many wonderful afternoons together, strolling around the Quarter, eating oysters, talking about our dreams and goals. One thing led to another, and our friendship grew to something more. Well, you know the rest." She gave a little shrug.

"I'm sorry about the way Remy acted toward your friends today," Shelley went on. She turned south onto Dumaine Street, heading toward the Faubourg Marigny neighborhood, where she and Remy lived. "I guess I should have warned you that he's been extra touchy lately. The pressure of opening the restaurant is getting to him, and then . . ." She let out a sigh and blew a flyaway strand of blond hair from her forehead.

"Is something else the matter?" Nancy asked.

"Well, Remy has a little sister, Delphine. She lives just outside New Orleans with their parents," Shelley explained. "She's just been diagnosed with a kidney condition. It's pretty serious, and the treatment is expensive."

"The poor thing," Bess murmured.

"Yes, it's terrible," Shelley said. "Remy's parents don't have a lot of money, and Remy has sunk almost all our savings into the restaurant," she went on. "Remember when you saw me talking to him before he left the café?" Nancy and Bess both nodded. "Well, he said he was gambling last night because he was hoping to win enough to help pay for the treatment."

"Why didn't he tell you sooner?" Nancy asked. She didn't want to pressure her friend, but half a million dollars was at stake.

"He thought I'd worry if I knew the police had questioned him," Shelley answered.

Nancy wished she could be as sure of that reason

as Shelley. But she couldn't ignore the fact that Remy had a motive for stealing the money. However, she decided to refrain from questioning her friend any further. Shelley was under enough pressure already.

"Check this place out," Bess said, cutting into Nancy's thoughts. Bess had stopped in front of a building near Bourbon Street and was reading the oval sign hanging over the entrance. "'New Orleans Historic Voodoo Museum.' I'd love to go in sometime."

Shelley's face brightened a little as she looked at the museum. "Voodoo has a long history in New Orleans, you know," she told Bess. "It's been practiced here as a respected religion for almost two hundred years—"

She broke off as the museum door opened and two young women stepped out. One of them had pale skin and flaming red hair that contrasted with her conservative gray pants and silk blouse. She stopped short when she saw Shelley.

"Well, if it isn't Shelley Maspero, the happiest blushing bride in Louisiana," she said. "How's married life treating you?"

Nancy was startled by the young woman's sarcastic tone and smirking expression. She and Shelley obviously knew each other, and it seemed just as obvious they were not friends.

"I, uh—" Shelley looked uncomfortable and avoided the woman's taunting gaze. "It's fine, Angela, just fine. How are you?"

"Getting better all the time," Angela answered,

still smirking. "You know, I was pretty bent out of shape when Remy broke up with me to be with you—"

Nancy caught the look of surprise Bess shot her. So *that* was why Angela seemed to hate Shelley so much.

"But I've found ways to cope with it," Angela went on. "As I'm sure you know, some people turn to voodoo to deal with their romantic competition."

She nodded toward the entrance of the Voodoo Museum, and her eyes narrowed to slits. "If I were you, Shelley, I'd watch your back."

Chapter
Four

ANGELA LEVELED an ice-cold look at Shelley that chilled Nancy to the bone. Shelley seemed so taken aback that she just stood there and gaped at Angela.

"Well, have a nice day," Angela said, her voice just as biting and sarcastic as before. She strode toward Bourbon Street and disappeared around the corner, her friend following uncertainly behind.

Bess bit her lower lip and gave Shelley a worried look. "Do you think she's planning to put some kind of curse on you?"

"No way," Shelley said, firmly shaking her head. "Angela Dixon is big on threats, but she'd never actually *do* anything to hurt Remy or me. She's just jealous. She and Remy were casually dating when he and I met. I mean, I feel bad for Angela, but she makes it sound as if I took Remy away from her. That's not the way it happened at all."

Nancy gazed in the direction Angela had gone, shaking away the uneasy feeling that had come over her. "It's not *your* fault that you and Remy were meant for each other," she said. "But speaking of Remy . . ."

"We'd better hurry if we want to get to the Royal Creole in time to taste his specialties," Shelley finished, her brown eyes lighting up. "Come on!"

An hour later Nancy, Bess, and Shelley emerged from the clapboard house on Frenchmen Street where Shelley and Remy had a second-story apartment. Shelley had called a taxi, which was waiting out front, but Bess hesitated on the sidewalk.

"Are you sure I look okay?" she asked. "My dress isn't too tight?"

Nancy glanced at the above-the-knee deep blue dress that hugged Bess's curves. "It's perfect," she decided. "Every guy at the Royal Creole is going to be paying more attention to you than the food."

"Don't say that!" Shelley chided good-naturedly. *"Nothing* is going to outshine Remy's cooking tonight." She let out a nervous laugh as she opened the taxi door and climbed in ahead of Nancy and Bess. "Not even three gorgeous, decked-out girls like us."

Nancy couldn't help feeling excited, too. This was Remy's big night, after all. The success of his restaurant could hinge on how smoothly everything went in the next few hours.

Ten minutes later the taxi stopped in front of a building on Royal Street, in the middle of the French Quarter. White shutters flanked the beveled glass windows overlooking the street, and gas lanterns flickered on either side of the entrance. Next to the doors was a plaque with The Royal Creole spelled out in elegant script letters.

"So far everything looks great," Bess commented. She hurried over to the entrance and tugged on the doorknob, then frowned. "It's locked."

Coming up next to Bess, Nancy peered through the window at the polished wood paneling, fluted columns, potted palms, and ceiling fans inside. The tables were set, but the lights were off, and Nancy didn't see a single person.

"Remy must be in the kitchen. He and the sous chefs must be in such a flurry that they forgot to leave the door open." She smiled, but Nancy could see the tension in her face. "I hope we got here before Randall Legarde did."

"Who's Randall Legarde?" Bess asked.

"Remy's financial backer," Shelley replied. "I don't think Mr. Legarde would be pleased to find himself locked out," she said. "We can go around to the kitchen through the rear courtyard garden and remind Remy to open up."

Nancy and Bess followed as Shelley hurried down a brick alleyway leading to a lush patio at the back of the restaurant. A handful of tables and gaslights were placed among azaleas, lemon trees, and lavender wisteria. French doors led to the inside dining room.

"It's gorgeous!" Bess exclaimed.

"Isn't it?" Shelley said with a proud smile. "The kitchen's over there." She started toward a low brick extension that jutted back from the restaurant beyond the French doors. A solid door and two windows were set into the brick wall of the extension, amid a thick row of red azaleas. "That's odd. The door is closed. Remy usually leaves the door open for fresh air when he's—"

Shelley stopped short as the bushes next to one of the kitchen windows shook. "Remy? Is that you?" she asked uncertainly.

As Nancy peered at the bushes, she caught sight of dark burnished skin and a brightly colored scarf. It was a woman, she realized with a start. What was she doing hiding among the bushes?

Nancy walked over to the azaleas and fixed the woman with a probing stare. "Can we help you with something?" she asked.

As the woman slowly emerged, Nancy saw that she was in her thirties, with a round face, full cheeks, and dark hair almost completely enveloped in her kerchief. Her heavyset figure was draped in a loose robe with a batik print on it.

"Ms. Thibaud!" Shelley said, looking at the woman in surprise.

"You know her?" Bess asked.

"Of course she knows me," the woman said, before Shelley could answer. "We *are* practically neighbors, after all."

She gave Shelley a nervous smile, but Shelley merely frowned. "Lisa Thibaud owns Thibaud's Creole Kitchen, a restaurant just down Royal Street," Shelley explained to Nancy and Bess. "A *competing* restaurant."

Turning back to Ms. Thibaud, Shelley planted

her hands on her hips and demanded, "What are you doing here?"

"No need to get in a huff, darlin'" Ms. Thibaud cut in smoothly. "I just stopped by to wish Remy good luck, but everything's locked up. And since he's not here . . ." She stepped casually away from the azaleas and headed back through the alleyway, toward the street. "Y'all be sure to pass along my good wishes."

Nancy could hardly believe it. Ms. Thibaud was acting as if it were perfectly normal to hide in someone's bushes. With an easy wave, Lisa Thibaud sauntered out of sight.

"Am I the only one who has the feeling she was up to something?" Bess asked, staring after the woman.

Shelley shook her head, looking worried. "Competition among restaurants is tough in New Orleans. Thibaud's Creole Kitchen used to be one of the hottest places in the Quarter, but Ms. Thibaud's business has fallen off in the last year or two. And now that Remy is opening the Royal Creole—"

"This place could take even more customers away from her," Nancy said.

"Exactly," Shelley said. "Remy already has a reputation for coming up with fresh, innovative twists on the Creole theme. I wouldn't put it past Ms. Thibaud to try to steal his ideas."

"We can't know for sure what she was doing hiding in the bushes," Nancy said. "But something tells me it *wasn't* to wish Remy good luck."

* * *

"Where *is* everyone?" Joe asked, peering through the front windows of the Royal Creole.

He, Frank, and Faye had taken Faye's car to the restaurant from the Gatlins' home, in the Garden District. But the restaurant looked deserted, and Joe didn't see Remy, Shelley, Nancy, or Bess anywhere. "Shelley *did* say she and Nancy and Bess would be here at four-thirty, right?" he asked.

"Yup," Frank said. But Joe noticed that Frank's attention was focused more on Faye than on the restaurant. Joe was beginning to be concerned that Frank was forgetting about the case.

Looks like it's up to me to keep an eye on Remy, Joe thought. *Someone* had to stay focused on the case—find out if Remy used cologne and look for any other clues that could link him to the stolen money.

Joe was glad when Nancy, Bess, and Shelley appeared from around the side of the restaurant. "Hi," he said, grinning. "We were beginning to wonder if you were lost in some kind of fourth dimension."

"We were in the courtyard. But maybe that *is* another dimension," Bess said, giggling. "That might explain what Lisa Thibaud was doing there."

"The competition," Nancy explained to Joe, Frank, and Faye. "Looks like she may have been trying to steal Remy's culinary secrets."

"Speaking of Remy," Faye said, looking around with curiosity. "Where is he?"

Shelley's face tightened with worry. "He should be here," she said. She nodded toward two men walking down the sidewalk toward them. Both were carrying chef's whites wrapped in dry-cleaner's plastic. "There are Jorge and Emil, the sous chefs. I don't understand. Prep work should be well under way by now. The dishwashers, waiters, and the hostess will probably be here any minute, not to mention Randall Legarde." Shelley looked more panicky every second. "How could Remy do this? And on opening night!"

Weird, thought Joe. Once again, Remy had taken off without any explanation even to his wife. "Makes you wonder, doesn't it?" he whispered to Frank. "I mean, what could be important enough to keep a guy away from his own restaurant on opening night?"

"Half a million dollars?" Frank whispered back. "I'm not sure what—"

"Shelley!"

Joe turned to see Remy running frantically toward them wearing his chef's whites, his face red and sweaty. "Thank goodness Mr. Legarde isn't here yet," he said breathlessly, looking up and down Royal Street. "Have y'all been waiting long? You're not going to believe the wild-goose chase I just went on. . . ."

He was talking a mile a minute, without giving anyone a chance to get a word in. Remy quickly fumbled with the keys in the lock, glancing over his shoulder at the two sous chefs who were standing nearby. "Jorge, Emil, we need to get back to work right away. I finished the praline pudding and the cake before I went out, but we still have to prep for—"

"Remy!" Shelley cut in, grabbing his arm. "What

happened? Why did you leave the restaurant in the first place?"

Remy finally calmed down enough to look at her. "I got a call from Bill Jacobson's assistant at the *New Orleans Morning Sun,*" he began.

"He's the most important food critic in New Orleans," Faye explained to Frank and Joe, sounding impressed. "A review from him can make or break a restaurant."

"Don't I know it," Remy said. "That's why I wasn't about to say no when his assistant told me Jacobson wanted to interview me right away at the newspaper office."

"I wonder why he wanted to interview you there?" Nancy asked. "Wouldn't it make more sense for him to come *here* to see the restaurant for himself?"

Remy nodded as he turned the key in the lock, then pulled the door open. "Absolutely. I was surprised, but as I said, I wasn't about to refuse him or question anything. I figured this interview was to be for an article and he'd show up another time to sample my food and to write a review."

"Bill Jacobson has a reputation for being quirky and mysterious," Shelley put in as they all hustled into the main dining room. "You never know when he'll show up, and he's not interested in just the food, either. He's even been known to appear before and after dining hours, to see how the kitchen is run."

"A guy like that must really keep everyone on their toes," Bess said, laughing.

"This time it wasn't so funny," Remy said, with a

dark frown. "I ran all the way over to the newspaper office, and Jacobson wasn't even there! No one at the paper knew a thing about any interview."

"Weird," Joe said. "It's almost as if the whole thing was a hoax."

"I can't worry about that now," Remy said. He hustled through the dining room and pushed through the swinging double doors to the kitchen. "Mr. Legarde will be here any minute, and I have to—"

Remy broke off, stopping just inside the doors. His face went completely white. "Oh, no!" he cried.

As Joe came in behind Remy, he caught a glimpse of stainless-steel counters, copper pots, and garlic, onions, and herbs hanging from the rafters. Colorful peppers were piled next to a butcher-block cutting board. A wire rack against the wall held small cakes and pastries, but Remy's eyes were focused on the counter next to it.

"Uh-oh," Joe murmured.

On the counter were the remains of a cake. One side of it still showed sculpted swirls of white frosting covering half a dozen tiers. The other side looked as if a grenade had exploded in it. Hunks of cake and frosting were everywhere.

"Your cake," Shelley breathed. "Someone's ruined it!"

Chapter

Five

NANCY FELT a wave of dread wash over her as she stared at the caved-in, demolished cake smeared across the rack and floor. "Something tells me this wasn't an accident," she said, thinking about their encounter earlier with Lisa Thibaud.

"Definitely not," Remy said, his voice shaking. "I put the finishing touches on the icing just before I left to meet Bill Jacobson at the *Morning Sun.*" He walked over to the ruined cake, his face pale and tight. "This was going to be the centerpiece of tonight's dessert cart. It took hours. There's no way I can make another one before we open."

"At least there are other desserts," Bess put in, nodding to the array of pastries, puddings, and cakes on the other shelves. She bit her lip, looking around uncertainly. "But is everything else okay?"

Remy glanced quickly around the kitchen. "Seems to be," he said. Throwing up his hands, he turned to Jorge and Emil, who were hovering uncertainly just inside the swinging doors. "We've got to prepare the shrimp and andouille stuffing for the artichokes, the sauce for the chicken Pontalba and the crawfish *boudin*. . . . I don't have time for this!"

Suddenly Remy was all action, and vegetables, sausages, seafood, and spices were flung on every counter in sight. Nancy was impressed by how fast and efficiently Remy and the sous chefs worked.

"I'll clean this mess up," Bess offered. She grabbed a broom hanging next to the sink and started sweeping up chunks of cake. Nancy was about to help, when she noticed the thoughtful expression on Faye Gatlin's face.

"Doesn't it seem odd—that phone call from Bill Jacobson's assistant coming just before the cake was smashed?" Faye asked. "And then Jacobson not being at the paper when Remy showed up?"

Nancy had been thinking the same thing, but it irked her just a little that Faye was the one to voice the suspicion.

"Makes you wonder if it was all a setup," Frank said, meeting Faye's gaze, "to lure Remy out of here so someone could sneak in and do some damage."

"That still doesn't tell us *who* would want to do this to Remy," Joe said as he and Shelley both scooped up gooey bits of frosting from the rack and tossed them into the trash.

Nancy exchanged quick glances with Bess and

Shelley, and all three of them said at once, "Lisa Thibaud."

"Lisa Thibaud?" Remy echoed. He looked up from the hot chili sauce he had just finished pouring into a ceramic container. "What does *she* have to do with this?"

As Nancy, Bess, and Shelley told him about finding Ms. Thibaud in the courtyard, red, angry-looking blotches appeared on Remy's cheeks. When the girls finished talking, Remy pounded his fist on the stainless-steel counter and burst out, "She would do anything to keep my restaurant from becoming a success!"

"She could be the person who called here, pretending to be Bill Jacobson's assistant," Bess suggested. "Then, once Remy was gone, she broke into the kitchen and—"

"Wham!" Joe slammed his palm with his other hand. "She came in for the kill. It makes sense, except for one thing. Why didn't she destroy anything else? I mean, if you want to ruin the competition, why not go all out? It's not like destroying a cake would ruin the opening night."

"Shelley, Bess, and I may have surprised her," Nancy said, thinking out loud. "She could have left the kitchen when she heard us at the front door."

"Then we cornered her in the courtyard before she could leave, so she hid," Shelley finished. "What a snake!"

Nancy went over to the kitchen's outside door to see if the lock had been tampered with. She turned the knob. "The door's open!" she exclaimed. "That's how she got in." She looked at Remy, puzzled. "But it was locked when we tried to get in earlier."

Remy laughed and went over to the door. "That's because this door has a special button you can push so that the door is open from the inside, but it's locked from the outside." He opened the door and pointed to a device in the side of the door frame. "See?"

Nancy bent down and checked the door. Sure enough, Remy was right. She tested the outside handle, and it didn't turn.

"I always use this lock during the day," Remy said. "But at night I double lock the door."

"That's a pretty easy lock to pick," Nancy pointed out. "It doesn't look like it was tampered with, though."

Nancy leaned past some canvas shopping bags hanging from a hook by the door and examined the two kitchen windows. "These are locked, too."

"So, how did Ms. Thibaud get in?" Frank wondered aloud.

"I have no idea," Remy said. He was standing near Nancy, and she saw him look down at the counter next to the windowsill and frown.

"Oh, no!" Rene exclaimed. "There are my recipe cards for stuffed artichokes and crawfish *boudin*. I was in such a hurry to go to the interview that I left them right here in plain sight. If Lisa Thibaud got a look at them . . ."

He stopped talking as two young men formally dressed in black pants and white button-down shirts appeared at the back door. "The waiters are here. Good." To Nancy, he said, "Look, I'm sorry, but as I said, I don't have time for this now."

Over the next few minutes, two more waiters and a couple of dishwashers showed up. While Remy hustled the waiters into the main dining room, Joe came over to Nancy. "You don't think Remy could have ruined the cake himself, do you?" he asked in a low voice. "I mean, there's no sign of forced entry. Maybe he's just acting like a victim so that Frank and I will stop focusing on him as a suspect in the theft from the riverboat casino."

"I don't know. He seemed genuinely upset about the cake. And we did catch Ms. Thibaud sneaking around," Nancy said, keeping her voice low enough so Shelley wouldn't hear. "Besides, the restaurant is so important to Remy. I don't think he'd do anything that might hurt his chances of success."

"Maybe not," Joe said. "Still, someone took that money."

Nancy listened carefully while Joe told her what had happened at Dupre's that afternoon. "So Paul blames Hugh Gatlin for the trouble he wound up in after Marsden embezzled from the club," she said. "Do you and Frank think that maybe Paul convinced the security guard to help him steal from the riverboat to get back at Mr. Gatlin?"

"Could be. That might explain what Mike was doing at Dupre's today. But Frank and I aren't writing off Remy as a suspect yet," Joe whispered. "Maybe you could help us out. Have you noticed him wearing any cologne since you've been here?"

"Something that could be that fruity, musky scent J. J. told you about?" Nancy thought for a moment, then shook her head. "I haven't smelled any cologne on him, but I'll try to check their apartment."

Before she could say anything more, Remy pushed back through the swinging doors into the kitchen. With him was one of the tallest men Nancy had ever seen, wearing an expensive-looking navy sports jacket with blue seersucker slacks.

"This is Randall Legarde, everyone," Remy said. "The man who made it possible for me to open the Royal Creole."

With all the chaos of the smashed cake, Nancy had completely forgotten that Remy's financial backer would be joining them for dinner. As she studied him, she guessed that Mr. Legarde was in his forties. With his muscular build, blond hair, and clean-cut good looks, he looked as if he'd once been a college football star. Everything about him radiated power.

After being introduced to Nancy, Bess, and the Hardys, Mr. Legarde turned to Remy and put his arm around the younger man. "Opening a fine local restaurant has always been a dream of mine," he told the group. "I never found the right chef—until my secretary at BayouTech told me about Remy. I went to one of Remy's cooking classes with her, and the rest is history."

As he clapped Remy around the shoulders, his blue eyes moved astutely over the kitchen. When his gaze landed on the remains of the cake, he let out a low whistle. "What happened?"

"We're still not sure," Remy admitted. Wiping his hands on his apron, he told Mr. Legarde about his suspicion that someone had sent him on a wild-goose chase to Bill Jacobson's office at the *Morning Sun* so that he or she could get inside the restaurant and sabotage the opening night.

"Sabotage? I don't like the sound of this, not a bit," Mr. Legarde said, frowning. "It's exactly the kind of incident that could affect our reviews. We don't want the food critics to think the Royal Creole is anything less than perfect—especially not Bill Jacobson."

"We're pretty sure the call was a hoax, and certainly not from anyone at the paper. Mr. Jacobson probably doesn't know anything about it," Shelley put in quickly.

"Well, let's keep it that way. I'd like to make sure word of this mishap doesn't go farther than this room," Mr. Legarde said. He spoke emphatically, looking from person to person. Nancy could tell the success of the restaurant was very important to him.

"You can count on us to keep quiet, Mr. Legarde," Frank assured him.

Remy had started to sauté a mixture of andouille sausage, red and green peppers, garlic, and some spices that sent an irresistible aroma through the kitchen. When he tossed in a handful of chopped shrimp, Nancy's mouth began to water.

"In the meantime," she said, sniffing the air, "I can't wait to try Remy's Creole specialties!"

"I can't believe I ate so much!" Bess exclaimed an hour and a half later. "Shrimp *remoulade,* blackened catfish, artichoke stuffed with shrimp and andouille sausage, crab cakes with roasted red pepper sauce . . ."

Frank was completely stuffed, too. But somehow he couldn't stop picking from the desserts Remy had brought for them to sample: flaming bananas, walnut bread pudding, crepes, and about four different puddings and cakes.

"Everything is delicious," Nancy said. "I'm not an expert, but I'd say the Royal Creole has gotten off to a fantastic start."

As Frank looked around, he had to agree. After a selection of entrees had been served to Mr. Legarde, friends, and other invited guests, Remy had declared the restaurant officially open. He invited in the crowd of diners who had been lining up on the sidewalk while the guests enjoyed their preview meal inside. Now the place was packed and everyone was eating, laughing, and talking with gusto.

"Even without his special cake, I'd say Remy has outdone himself," Mr. Legarde said. He scooped up the last of his crème brûlée, then gave a satisfied smile. "Every dish was outstanding."

"I knew Remy could do it," Shelley said. She'd been grinning from ear to ear ever since they sat down. Obviously she'd forgotten that her husband was a suspect in the theft from the riverboat, Frank thought, but *he* hadn't. As the waiter arrived to clear away their plates and coffee cups, Frank checked his watch.

"Sorry to eat and run," he said, putting his

napkin on the table, "but Joe, Faye, and I have to get going if we want to make the seven forty-five cruise on the *Delta Princess.*"

"Y'all are welcome to join us," Faye added, turning to Nancy, Bess, and Shelley.

"Sounds great!" Bess said.

Nancy nodded her agreement, but Shelley held back. "You two go ahead," she told Nancy and Bess. "I want to stay here in case Remy needs help. We'll meet you back at our place later."

After saying good night, Frank, Joe, Faye, Nancy, and Bess all piled into Faye's white hatchback and drove to the *Delta Princess* pier.

"Wow," said Bess, staring up at the huge riverboat, with its ornate railings, two-tiered decks, and double paddle wheel at the stern. Bright light spilled from the windows as people made their way up the ramp and inside the floating casino. "It looks like something straight out of an old movie."

"That's the way Daddy wanted it," Faye said proudly. "The *Princess* is an authentic re-creation of a turn-of-the-century steamboat."

Frank gave a nod, but he wasn't nearly as interested in the boat's history as he was in getting to the bottom of the theft. Joining the groups of tourists, he, Joe, Faye, Nancy, and Bess boarded the floating casino. They found themselves in a carpeted interior hallway with arched doorways leading to the gaming rooms and the Dixieland Jazz Bar.

"Mike's probably in the gaming rooms. I'll get him so he can show you two where the safe is," Faye said to Frank and Joe.

"Bess and I can wait in there." Nancy nodded

toward the jazz bar. "That way we can keep an eye on Danielle *and* enjoy the music."

Soon after Nancy and Bess went into the jazz club, Mike emerged from the gaming rooms. For a brief second, he gave Frank and Joe a hooded glance. But it was quickly replaced by his usual boyish smile. "Evenin', y'all," Mike said easily. "How's it goin'?"

"Not bad—considering someone tried to kill me at Dupre's this afternoon," Joe said. He crossed his arms over his chest and stared pointedly at Mike. "The person looked a little like you, actually."

"Me?" Mike flashed Joe a look of total innocence Frank didn't trust for a second. "What would *I* be doing at Dupre's?"

Good question, thought Frank. But he could tell Mike wasn't going to give them a straight answer, so he changed the subject. "Could we see the safe?" Frank asked.

Mike led Frank, Joe, and Faye from the gaming rooms and onto the deck. He headed aft, where metal stairs rose to the upper deck.

"Is this where J. J. Johnson was when he heard the thief run by?" Faye asked, glancing up and down the upper deck.

Mike nodded. "The safe's right through here."

Frank, Joe, and Faye followed as Mike entered the upper-level cabin and went down a carpeted hallway. He stopped at a door about a dozen feet down the hall and punched a code into an electronic pad on the wall. Then he singled out a key from his keychain and unlocked the door. "The alarm's off," he said, pushing the door open.

The first thing Frank saw was a wall safe whose door had been twisted halfway off its hinges. On the floor below it was a slightly damaged framed photograph of the *Delta Princess*. Frank guessed it had covered the safe before the break-in.

"Mr. Gatlin had a new safe installed in another office," Mike said. "Feel free to look around here as long as you like. I'll be right outside on deck while y'all do your thing, but I need to lock up when you're finished. Even though there's nothing of value here anymore, the police want the room off-limits. Anyway, if you need me, give a yell."

"Right," Joe muttered under his breath as Mike went back through the door to the deck. "I'll be sure to call—next time I want my head bashed in."

"I don't trust the guy, either," Frank said, giving Joe a warning look. "But until we have a chance to talk to Mr. Gatlin, we have to depend on him to help us."

"We can talk to Daddy in the morning," Faye added. "But in the meantime"—she gestured around the room—"don't we have work to do?"

Frank gave Faye a sideways look, something he'd found himself doing all evening. Not only was she gorgeous and charming, but she also had an awesome way of staying focused on what was important. He couldn't help being impressed.

While Joe and Faye looked over the rest of the office, Frank inspected the safe. The locking mechanism had been destroyed, and there were traces of plastic explosives on the safe and surrounding area, but Frank didn't see anything to indicate who had planted the explosive. "Whoever broke in did a good job of covering his tracks," he said.

"Nothing unusual here, either." Joe straightened up from the desk and shook his head in disgust. "Well, this was a bust. We might as well get Mike to lock up again." He headed out the door, and a moment later, Frank heard him say, "Hey—where's Mike?"

Frank and Faye went out to the upper deck, where Joe was looking back and forth. "He's not here."

"Not in sight, anyway," Faye added. She stepped past Joe onto the deck. "I'll look around for him."

"I'll come, too," Frank spoke up quickly—too quickly, Joe thought. Before he could comment, Frank added, "You'd better stay near the safe until we find him, Joe."

"Mmm" was all Joe said. He shot Frank a sideways glance before heading back down the hallway to the office where the safe was.

When Frank turned back to Faye, she was staring at him with liquid green eyes that drew him, once again, like a magnet. Suddenly he was intensely aware of the evening breeze on his arms, the smell of the river, and the screech of gulls hovering over the steamboat.

"Well . . ." Frank shook himself, forcing himself to concentrate on finding Mike. "Let's try the back of the boat," he suggested. "That's where J. J. said the thief climbed down. Even if Mike's not there—"

"Maybe we'll find something the police overlooked," Faye finished.

Frank couldn't help grinning at her as they headed aft. "Are you sure you haven't done any investigating before? You're a natural."

Faye's rich laugh rang in the night air, mixing with the rhythmic swoosh of the paddle wheel. "What can I say? I'm a fast learner," she told him. "I guess it helps to work with someone you've got a special chemistry with." Her voice dropped a notch as she added, "Don't you think so?"

She slowed her step, staring at him with such sparkling promise that Frank couldn't resist the urge to touch her. Reaching out, he gently stroked her long dark hair. "Definitely," he whispered.

Frank felt as if a force of nature was pulling him closer to Faye. His mouth hovered just above hers, and she closed her eyes and slipped her arms around him.

He was about to kiss her when he heard a man say, "We've got to talk."

Frank jolted to attention, straightening away from Faye. The guy speaking was Mike Keyes! Frank couldn't hear anyone else, but Mike sounded urgent.

There was a short pause before Mike continued. "The Riverside construction site, tomorrow morning at nine o'clock," he said. "Be there—or else."

Faye's eyes widened. Frank pressed a finger to her lips to keep her from saying anything. "Stay here," he whispered.

Frank and Faye were standing in the shadow of metal stairs that rose to the roof of the *Delta Princess*. From what Frank could tell, Mike's voice had come from the very back of the riverboat, behind the stairs. Frank hadn't heard a second person. Could Mike have been using a phone? he wondered.

Frank moved slowly aft, skirting around the stairs and keeping his eyes glued to the back of the boat. Straight ahead, the aft railing was a black silhouette against the moonlit night. As he turned the corner, he saw that the aft deck was in shadow. He spotted a deeper shadow against the cabin wall—some kind of storage container, he guessed.

Suddenly, the hairs rose on the back of Frank's neck. Something was wrong—he could feel it. But standing by the railing, he saw nothing other than shadows and a glimpse of water being pulled around in the huge double paddle wheel just below. But a sixth sense told him to stay on his toes.

Frank kept to the railing, his eyes focused on the thick shadows surrounding the storage bin. He couldn't see anything. Slowly, he shifted his attention to the deck on the other side of the riverboat. Maybe Mike had slipped around that way.

"What . . . ?" Frank jumped at the sound of footsteps next to the storage bin. Before he could turn around, he felt a shoulder shove into his back with the force of a Mack truck.

"Hey!" Frank yelled. He threw his arms out, but he was already flying over the aft railing. In a single terrifying glance, he caught sight of the paddle wheel churning relentlessly around just below him. In a second he was going to fall right into it!

Chapter

Six

Nancy stiffened, tightening her grip on the railing of the lower-level deck. "Bess! Did you hear that cry?"

The two of them had just come out of the jazz club for some fresh air. Now it appeared they were getting more than they bargained for.

"It sounds like someone's in trouble!" Bess exclaimed, and stared toward the rear of the riverboat, where the shout had come from. "Do you think someone fell overboard?"

"I hope not," Nancy answered. She gazed aft but couldn't see anything past the metal steps that rose to the riverboat's upper deck. "We'd better check it out, though."

As she ran toward the boat's stern, Nancy kept glancing over the railing, but she saw only branches and garbage floating on the sluggish waters—no people. At least, not yet . . .

Suddenly she heard someone pounding down the metal steps from the upper level. Seconds later a tall young man with bulging muscles and a freckled face shot from the stairs and onto the lower deck, half a dozen feet in front of her and Bess. He was holding a cellular phone, Nancy saw. A badge pinned to his suit jacket read Security. When his eyes fell on Nancy and Bess, he slowed his pace, and his eyes narrowed. Then the man folded the phone, shoved it into his back pocket, and disappeared inside the lower level of the riverboat.

"During dinner tonight, Joe told me that he and Frank suspect that a security guard on the *Delta Princess* could have been involved in the theft," Nancy murmured, frowning. "Some guy named Mike Keyes."

"You think that was him?" Bess asked.

"I don't know, but he was running *away* from the shout," Nancy said. "We'd better make sure no one's hurt. Come on!"

Nancy took the steps two at a time, with Bess right behind her. As she burst onto the upper deck, she whipped her head left and right—then gasped.

"Faye!" Nancy exclaimed.

Faye Gatlin was bending over the railing at the boat's stern, just above the riverboat's immense paddle wheel. Her face was red and sweaty, and she could barely keep her feet on the deck floor. It looked as if she was struggling to hold on to something—or someone.

"It's Frank," Faye managed to get out. "I'm going to lose him!"

Nancy was at the railing in a flash. As she bent over next to Faye, she saw Frank dangling below. Nancy felt a knot of fear in her stomach when she saw how close he was to the rotating slats of the paddle wheel.

"I'm slipping!" he shouted. His face was pale, his fingers white where they clutched Faye's wrist.

Nancy was already stretching her hand downward. As it closed around Frank's wrist, she felt his weight start to pull her over.

"I've got you, Nan," Bess said.

Nancy felt as if her arms might yank out of their sockets, but somehow she, Faye, and Bess managed to pull Frank back on deck. He immediately sank to his knees, sucking in deep breaths of air. "Thanks," he gasped. "If you hadn't been there, I'd be—"

"Don't say it," Faye interrupted. Nancy didn't miss the electricity in Faye's eyes as she looked at Frank. "You're fine. That's what's important."

"What happened?" Bess asked. "We heard you cry out. And then a security guard practically ran us down while we were coming this way."

"Tall, brown hair, kind of boyish looking," Nancy supplied. "Joe mentioned a guard you two are keeping an eye on. Do you think it was him?"

Frank nodded as he reached up to massage his shoulder. "Mike Keyes. That sounds like him, all right. Faye and I overheard someone talking about a rendezvous tomorrow morning. It sounded like

Mike, so I went to check it out," Frank explained. "I guess he saw me before I saw him. The next thing I knew I was taking a one-way trip over the railing."

"The guy we saw was carrying a cellular phone," Nancy said. She shivered as she looked at the paddle wheel's blades plunging beneath the water, over and over again.

"Hey! Here you guys are." Joe appeared in one of the doorways leading out to the deck from the upper level. "Mike locked everything up, so we can . . ." His voice trailed off, and his smile faded as he looked from face to face. "What happened?" he asked.

Nancy, Bess, Frank, and Faye all chimed in with the story. As Joe listened, his jaw tightened and his hands balled into fists at his side. "Mike told me he hadn't even seen you and Faye," Joe said angrily. "He said he just came to find us because he thought we might be finished. Said he couldn't stick around because he needed to keep an eye on things in the gaming rooms. After locking up and reactivating the alarm, he left."

"What a liar," Bess said, shaking her head in disgust.

"If Mike *was* mixed up in last night's theft, he must have had a partner who actually took the money," Frank said. "That could be the person he's planning to meet."

"Paul or Danielle Dupre?" Faye guessed, raising an eyebrow. "Joe, you said you thought it was Mike nosing around their place this afternoon."

"Could be," Joe said.

"Or maybe Remy." Frank said. "With any luck, we'll find out tomorrow morning. Joe and I are definitely going to stake out the rendezvous." Turning to Faye, he asked, "Do you know where the Riverside construction site is?"

"Sure," she answered. "Riverside is going to be a gambling complex down by the water, on Lafayette Street, in the Warehouse District. I have to work tomorrow—we're doing inventory at the store. But you and Joe can take my car."

Joe turned to Nancy and Bess and said, "The stakeout won't take long. We could meet you guys for lunch afterward."

"Sounds like a good plan," Bess said, grinning. "We're going sightseeing in the Garden District with Shelley in the morning, but we could meet afterward."

"How about if we meet at Jackson Square at noon?" Nancy suggested. "We can decide where to go then."

"Too bad I can't join y'all," Faye said, "but I'll be working until late. I only work part-time, but sometimes the hours are crazy. Anyway"—she looked around the group—"why don't we go downstairs now to hear some jazz?"

Even though Faye spoke to the group, Nancy noticed her eyes were focused exclusively on Frank. As the rest of the group started down the stairs and back toward the jazz club, Bess lingered behind with Nancy. "Are you okay, Nan?" she asked.

Nancy shrugged. "Sure. Why wouldn't I be?"

"Well, it's kind of hard not to notice something's going on between Frank and Faye," Bess said. "And you and Frank have always had your own special chemistry."

Nancy looked at Bess in surprise. "I should have known nothing gets past the Bess Marvin radar when it comes to romance," she said, laughing. "But seriously . . ." She paused, forcing herself to examine how she felt. "I guess it *is* a little weird," she admitted, "but Frank and I are friends—good friends—and we've both decided we can't be any more than that."

"So, you're not jealous?" Bess asked.

Nancy brushed a lock of reddish blond hair off her face before answering. "Well, maybe a little," she admitted. "Frank's been paying so much attention to Faye that I miss him—as a friend. But if he's happy with Faye, then I'm happy for him."

As she spoke, Nancy realized that she meant every word. "Come on," she said, smiling at Bess. "Let's find everyone else."

Joe leaned back in his chair in the Dixieland Jazz Bar, tapping his foot to the upbeat music. J. J. Johnson and the brass band were terrific, and Danielle had a strong voice with a wide range.

Well, he thought, he and Frank still didn't know who had taken the money from the safe the night before, or what Mike Keyes was up to, but there was an up side to the case. At least they got to listen to great music!

Danielle's voice grew louder while the trumpet,

saxophone, banjo, and slide trombone all built to a wild climax. When the song ended, everyone in the club clapped and cheered.

"Thanks," Danielle said into her microphone. "We're going to take a short break now. . . ."

Joe watched idly while Danielle stood chatting with J. J. and the other band members. He was just taking a swallow of his soft drink when he saw her expression change abruptly. As she looked toward the entrance to the Dixieland Jazz Bar, her smile turned to a dark, brooding frown.

Joe followed her gaze and spotted Mike walking on the deck outside. Moments later Danielle hurried out of the club, heading toward the bow—the same direction Mike had taken.

Hmm, thought Joe. What's going on?

"I'll be right back," he said to everyone else at his table. He jumped to his feet and hurried from the jazz bar onto the deck. Danielle was just disappearing around the front of the boat.

The soles of Joe's loafers squeaked against the deck as he jogged to the bow and peered around to the boat's other side. Danielle had caught up to Mike. The lights in the windows of the gaming rooms illuminated the deck, and Joe could see that the two were talking intently. They were too far away for Joe to hear them, but he didn't get the feeling they were talking about the weather.

He was just wondering how he could get close enough to hear them, when the two parted. Mike continued aft along the lower deck, but Danielle stayed where she was, leaning against the railing and staring out at the Mississippi River. The frenzied sounds of voices and machines in the gaming rooms burst through the windows behind her.

Here goes, Joe thought. "Hi," he said, flashing her a smile. "What a coincidence, running into you out here."

Danielle looked at him, then looked back at the water. "Mmm," was all she said.

"Didn't I just see you talking to Mike Keyes?" Joe pressed.

That got her attention. Danielle shifted her gaze from the water to give him a wary once-over. "Afraid not," she said slowly. "I just thought I'd get some fresh air while I'm on break. Can't say as I've seen Mike."

"Oh, really?" Joe said, not bothering to hide his doubt. "I could have sworn—"

Danielle gave an exaggerated whistle as she glanced at her watch. "It's later than I thought. I really should be getting back to the club," she said, giving Joe an insincere smile. She turned and hurried down the deck.

Joe glared after her. Danielle was good at sidestepping questions, he thought. But one way or another, he and Frank were going to get the answers they needed.

"What a night," Bess said a few hours later. "I'm beat." She yawned as she got out of the taxi that she and Nancy had taken from the riverboat dock to the clapboard house where Shelley and Remy lived.

"It looks like Shelley and Remy are home, too,"

Nancy said. She nodded toward the lighted windows of the second-floor apartment. "I wonder how the rest of the night went at the restaurant?"

Using the key Shelley had given her and Bess, Nancy unlocked the outside door, and she and Bess went upstairs. "Hello?" Bess called, as they entered the apartment.

"Remy?" Shelley hurried into the foyer from the adjoining living room. When she saw Nancy and Bess, the expectant smile faded on her lips. "Oh. Hi, you guys. I thought maybe you were Remy."

"He's not here?" Bess asked, glancing at the empty couch and chair in the living room.

Shelley shook her head. "I left him at the restaurant a few hours ago. I felt that I was just getting in the way, so I came home to finish a paper I'm working on." She glanced at the clock on the wall, then frowned. "Remy should be home by now. His parents and little sister have already called twice to find out how opening night went."

"Maybe he got held up. Opening night is a big deal, after all," Bess said.

"Oh, I know that. But Remy called forty-five minutes ago to say he was leaving. It only takes about fifteen minutes to get here." Shelley hurried back into the living room, reached for the phone on the coffee table, and punched in some numbers. After a few moments, she hung up again. "There's no answer at the restaurant."

She shot a nervous glance from Nancy to Bess. "I know I'm being paranoid, but would you mind going back to the restaurant with me? After what happened before . . ."

"It's better to be safe than sorry," Nancy finished. "We'll be glad to go."

Fifteen minutes later, they were standing in front of the front entrance to the Royal Creole. "The door's locked, and the dining room's dark," Shelley said, peering through the beveled glass.

As Nancy bent close to the doors, she saw a yellow glow shining through the glass panes of the swinging doors to the kitchen. "There's a light on in the back," she said.

"So he *is* here," Shelley murmured. "But why didn't he answer the phone?"

Frowning, she hurried around to the rear courtyard, with Nancy and Bess close behind. The gaslights were still lit, and the kitchen door was wide open. Bright light spilled from it onto the patio tables outside.

"Remy?" Shelley called. She ran lightly up to the doorway—then stopped so short that Nancy almost knocked right into her.

As soon as Nancy glanced inside the kitchen, her heart stopped. "Oh, no . . ." she breathed.

The kitchen looked as if a hurricane had ripped through it. Pots, pans, broken dishes, and food were everywhere. Nancy gasped when her eyes fell on a twisted figure wearing chef's whites, lying perfectly still on the floor inside the door.

It was Remy.

Chapter

Seven

REMY!" SHELLEY CRIED. Her face filled with fear, she dropped to her knees and shook him.

Bess's hand flew to her mouth. "Oh my gosh! Is he—"

"Oooooh" Remy let out a groan as he stirred, then opened his eyes a crack.

Seeing him move, Nancy was finally able to let out the breath she'd been holding. "Thank goodness he's alive," she murmured.

Remy blinked a few times before his eyes focused on them. "Shelley? What are you doing here?" he asked groggily.

"I was worried when you didn't come home," Shelley said as she helped him sit up. "I thought I was being paranoid, but—"

"What happened, Remy?" Nancy cut in gently.

"I—I'm not sure," he answered. He raked a

hand through his dark hair, then slowly pushed himself to his feet. "I was going to turn off the gaslights and lock the courtyard gate before leaving. I remember reaching to turn off the kitchen lights, and then—" He touched the back of his head and winced. "I guess someone knocked me out."

Remy's expression was grim as he surveyed the wreckage of the kitchen. "Not again!" He groaned. "What's going on?"

"That's what I'd like to know," Nancy said. "You didn't see or hear anything unusual before you were knocked out?"

Remy shook his head. "No, but I wasn't paying close attention. I was going over every detail of this evening. I was thinking about which recipes I was going to use in an article I'm going to write. Frankly," he added a bit sheepishly, "I was too busy daydreaming and congratulating myself on how well everything went tonight. . . ."

His voice trailed off as he turned to look out to the courtyard. "Oh, no," he breathed. "That's Bill Jacobson! I recognize him from a photo that was part of a magazine profile I read on him."

"Hello," a voice called from outside. Glancing through the open door, Nancy saw a short, rotund man with a full beard entering the courtyard.

Remy's eyes flickered over the mounds of pots, pans, and food strewn across the floor. "I can't let him see this mess, but if he knows I'm here, I'll have to show him around." He jumped back from the doorway, ducking out of sight.

"What are we going to do?" Shelley asked in a terrified whisper.

"I don't know, but we'd better move fast," Nancy said. "He's heading this way!"

Taking a deep breath, Shelley hurried into the courtyard, then closed the kitchen door behind her. "Hello?" she called. "I'm sorry, sir, but we're closed for the night."

"I know it's late, but I'm something of a restaurant enthusiast," Nancy heard Jacobson say. "As long as I'm here, I don't suppose it would be possible to take a quick look around?"

Nancy held her breath. "The owner's not here, and he'd kill me if I let anyone in," Shelley said, clearly not letting on that she knew the "restaurant enthusiast" was actually a renowned restaurant critic. "Perhaps I could make you a reservation for another night?"

There was a short pause before Jacobson answered. "I'm afraid that won't be possible. My schedule is unpredictable." He gave a mysterious laugh, then said, "But I'll be back."

Jacobson said good night, then Nancy heard him walk away. As his footsteps faded, Remy let out a sigh of relief. Shelley came back into the kitchen a moment later.

"That was close," she breathed. "Too close."

Nancy frowned as she looked over the wreckage of the kitchen. "To tell you the truth, I'm more worried about what happened here than about Bill Jacobson," she said.

"Someone is out to get me, and I know who it is," Remy said angrily. "Lisa Thibaud! First she ruined my cake, and now—this. Shelley is right. Lisa probably got scared away the first time before she could do too much damage. Tonight she came back and finished what she started."

"What about Angela Dixon?" Bess suggested.

Remy and Shelley both shook their heads. "Shelley told me what Angela said when you ran into her outside the museum today, but I still don't believe she'd do this," Remy said. "She's got a sharp tongue, but she's not violent."

Nancy wished she could be sure of that, but she knew from experience that jealousy sometimes made people do terrible things. "Angela still seems steamed that you broke up with her," she told Remy. "And she did tell Shelley she should watch her back."

Remy frowned but said nothing. He bent to scoop up some canvas bags scattered across the floor, then slipped them onto a hook next to the door. "That's odd. One of my shopping bags is missing," he said. "The giveaway bag from the National Culinary Institute's convention in San Francisco last year."

"Maybe whoever knocked you out used the bag to take something from the restaurant," Nancy suggested. "We'd better do a thorough check."

For the next ten minutes, Remy sifted through the mess in the kitchen and looked quickly through the rest of the restaurant. "Nothing else is missing," he said when he was done. He shook his head, a brooding, intense expression in his eyes.

"It's going to take hours to put this place back together," he muttered. "But all I feel like doing now is telling Lisa Thibaud to lay off or I'll go to the police!"

Nancy still wasn't convinced Ms. Thibaud was the culprit. Remy was still a suspect in the theft from the riverboat casino, after all. Nancy couldn't ignore the possibility that these attacks were somehow related to that case. But it couldn't hurt to check out all the possibilities. "Maybe *you'll* be busy cleaning, Remy, but that doesn't mean *we* can't pay her a visit," Nancy said, grinning at Bess and Shelley. "Tomorrow morning, our first stop will be Thibaud's Creole Kitchen."

"So, you think Mike Keyes may have had something to do with stealing the money?" Hugh Gatlin asked Frank and Joe Sunday morning.

Faye had already left for work at Michaud's, but the Hardys and Mr. Gatlin were eating a breakfast of strong New Orleans coffee, eggs, and spiced corn bread at the Gatlins' house. It was the first chance Frank and Joe had had to bring Faye's father up to date on all that had happened the day before. When they had mentioned their suspicion that Mike was the person who'd tried to hit Joe with a piece of wrought-iron railing and push Frank over the side of the *Delta Princess,* Mr. Gatlin had become very worried.

"Mike's an old family friend," he said, his expression grave. "His father and I go back over thirty years, since high school days."

"Nevertheless, we have to consider the possibility," Frank told him, after taking a bite of corn bread. "That's why Joe and I are going to stake out the rendezvous we heard Mike arrange on the riverboat casino last night."

Mr. Gatlin's round stomach butted against the table edge as he leaned forward to reach for the coffeepot. "I spoke to Detective Rollins down at the police station this morning. His men spoke to Mike and don't seem to think he's involved," he said, frowning, as he poured himself another cup of coffee.

"What about Remy Maspero?" Joe asked. "We know the police spoke to him. Have they found anything on him?"

"Nothing concrete. They're continuing to keep an eye on him," Mr. Gatlin answered. "After hearing what happened at Dupre's yesterday, I'll talk to Detective Rollins about Paul, as well. Seems to me *he's* the one we're after. He and that niece of his—what's her name?"

"Danielle," Joe supplied. "Frank and I are checking both of them out, too—after we see what happens at the Riverside construction site."

When Joe looked across the table at him, Frank could see a look of impatience in his eyes. As usual, Joe was itching to get going.

"Speaking of which . . ." Frank gulped down the last of his coffee, then got to his feet. "We'd better leave if we want to find a place to hide before the rendezvous. It's after eight, and Mike said he was going to meet the other person at nine."

Mr. Gatlin reached over to the sideboard and picked up car keys, which he tossed to Frank. "Faye left these for you. She takes the streetcar to work. Good luck."

"Talk about bad luck!" Joe kicked at the rear left tire of Faye's white hatchback twenty minutes later. "Why do we have to get a flat tire now?"

"We don't exactly have time to sit around and debate the question," Frank said. He jogged to the back of the car and used the key to open the hatchback. "Help me get out the jack."

Joe kept checking his watch as they took off the flat tire. "Come *on,*" he urged under his breath, as much to himself as to Frank.

The Hardys worked as fast as they could, but it still seemed to take forever before the spare tire was in place and they could get going again. Joe hopped behind the wheel, hitting the gas pedal as soon as Frank pulled the passenger door closed. "Riverside, here we come," he said.

Leaving behind the sumptuous homes of the Garden District, Joe steered Faye's car into the Warehouse District, past industrial buildings that had been converted to galleries, boutiques, and restaurants. As he neared the river on Lafayette Street, Joe spotted a block-long area surrounded by a plywood barrier. Over the top of the barrier he could see half a dozen bulldozers, backhoes, and cranes. There was a chain-link gate about twenty feet wide at one end of the construction site.

"This must be the place," he said, pointing. "I guess there's no work going on, since it's Sunday."

He parked the car, and he and Frank jogged over

to the chain-link gate. Joe frowned when he saw that the gate had been pulled open a few feet. The heavy chain and padlock used for securing it had been cut clean through.

"Looks like someone got here ahead of us," Frank said grimly. "Careful, little brother. Mike and whomever he's meeting could be anywhere."

Joe nodded. As he and Frank entered the site, Joe carefully looked around the entire area. A huge pit some thirty feet deep had been dug at the center of the site. Heavy metal I beams had been sunk into the periphery of the pit, and mountains of earth were heaped outside it. There were rutted tire tracks from the entrance to half a dozen different piles of earth, but Joe didn't see anyone.

"This way," Joe mouthed. All his senses were on red alert as he moved slowly toward the closest mound, ready to inspect it. A huge dump truck was parked next to it, partially filled with clumps of red-brown earth. Joe's eyes darted over the site, searching for any movement.

They were about twenty feet from the dump truck when Joe heard the roar of an engine starting.

"Hey! What . . . ?"

His eyes flew to the cab of the truck, but it was empty. Before he could take another step, a shiny black Jeep tore from around the back of the truck.

"It's heading straight for us!" Frank yelled.

Joe dove to the side a split second after his brother. His left shoulder and cheek slammed into the ground as the Jeep tore right past him and Frank. The wheels sent muddy clumps of earth and rocks showering over the Hardys. Joe looked up in time to see the Jeep crash into the chain-link gate, sending it flying open. The Jeep screeched around onto Lafayette Street and disappeared from sight.

"You okay, Joe?"

Joe turned to see his brother scrambling to his feet, wiping dirt from his hands. "Fine, no thanks to that yahoo," Joe answered. "I was too busy getting a mouthful of dirt to see the guy. Was it Mike?"

"Maybe. Or the person he was meeting," Frank said. "I couldn't tell, but"—he turned grimly toward the dump truck—"if anyone else is back there, they definitely know we're here."

Joe dropped into a defensive crouch as did Frank, and the two of them slowly moved the rest of the way to the truck. They angled around the cab, and Joe let out his breath in relief.

"All clear," he said.

He saw dirt and more dirt, piled at the edge of the yawning construction pit. Tire tracks from the Jeep stopped close to the dump truck. Joe was going over to examine them when he saw a pair of black snakeskin cowboy boots behind the dump truck. The boots were attached to jean-clad legs that were perfectly still.

"Uh-oh," he said. "Looks like I spoke too soon." He jumped forward, then stopped short when he saw the person's face. "It's Mike!"

Mike was propped up against the truck, and his eyes were closed. The hair at the back of his head was matted with sticky red blood that oozed down his clothes into a pool on the ground next to him. After one glance, Joe had to swallow hard to keep his breakfast from coming up.

Frank pressed a finger to Mike's neck, then looked at Joe with sober eyes. "He's dead."

Chapter

Eight

FRANK'S STOMACH churned as he stared at Mike's blank, pale face and the pool of blood that stained the dirt. It wasn't the first dead person he'd ever seen, but that didn't make it any easier.

"Check this out," Joe said. He dropped to his knees next to a rock in the dirt a few feet from Mike. The rock was about half a foot long, with a sharp protrusion on one end. "See that dark stain on the pointy end?"

"Blood," Frank said. "Looks like we found the murder weapon. Now, all we have to do is figure out who the killer is. We know he drives a black Jeep, and if he agreed to meet Mike at a deserted construction site, it's a pretty safe bet that it wasn't to have a Boy Scout meeting."

"Which brings us back to the money that was stolen from the *Delta Princess*," Joe put in. "If

Mike *was* working with the person who stole the money, maybe that person double-crossed Mike and killed him so that he could keep Mike's share."

That made sense, Frank thought. "Paul Dupre?" he suggested. "Maybe Danielle, too. You did see her and Mike talking together on the riverboat last night."

"Then she definitely lied to me about it," Joe said as he and Frank strode back toward Lafayette Street. "I guess our next step is finding out whether Danielle or Paul drives a black Jeep, huh?"

"That would connect them to Mike's murder," Frank said, his tone thoughtful, "but not to the theft of the half-million from the *Delta Princess*. Unless we find the money or some proof that Paul or Danielle broke into the safe, we can't pin the theft on either of them."

As they came out onto Lafayette Street, Frank spotted a pay phone across the street. "We'd better call the police," he said. "We'll have to tell them what we know, and——"

"Isn't that Mike's car?" Joe cut in. He pointed farther up Lafayette Street, at a beat-up red convertible parked at the curb. When Frank nodded, Joe raised an eyebrow and said, "The top is down. That's practically an invitation to look around."

"Definitely," Frank said, grinning. "Go for it, Joe. I'll be there in a sec."

Frank spent the next few minutes talking to Detective Steve Rollins. "Hardy, eh?" the detective said, after Frank gave his name. "You're the kids Hugh Gatlin called in."

"That's right," Frank told him. Ignoring the

reference to him and Joe as "kids," he gave a quick rundown of their suspicions of Mike Keyes and what they'd found at the Riverside construction site. The detective didn't sound happy to learn that Frank and Joe had sneaked into the site—*or* that Mike was dead.

"I'll send a couple of men over there right away," Detective Rollins said over the line. "You two stay put until they get there."

"Sure thing," Frank told him. He hung up, then jogged up the street to Mike's car. Joe was just pulling something from beneath the driver's seat.

"Look at this," Joe said. He held up a white canvas bag with a chef's cap printed on it.

As Frank stared at the chef's cap, he had the feeling he'd seen it before, but he couldn't think where. " 'National Culinary Institute, San Francisco, June fourth through seventh,' " he said, reading the print beneath the logo. "Hey!" he said, snapping his fingers. "This is the bag we saw in the security tape from the *Delta Princess!*"

"The one Remy had?" Joe took another look at the bag, then nodded. "You could be right. What's it doing in *Mike's* car?"

Frank had been wondering the same thing, and so far he'd only come up with one possible answer. "Maybe Remy worked with Mike to steal the money from the riverboat," he suggested. "Nancy told us last night he needs cash to help pay for his sister's medical treatments."

"Yeah, but that doesn't explain why Mike would have been at Dupre's yesterday," Joe said. "Or why

Danielle would lie about talking to Mike on the *Delta Princess* last night. We need more to go on."

He flipped open the glove compartment and looked around inside. "Nothing much in here except Mike's car registration," he said, holding up a clear plastic folder with a card inside. "This says he lives at 2316 Esplanade Avenue, Apartment three."

Frank saw the gleam in Joe's eyes and knew exactly what he was thinking. "I would be great if we could take a look around Mike's place," Frank said. "We might be able to find out exactly what he's been up to—"

"And who he's been up to it *with,*" Joe added.

"There's just one problem," Frank said. "I told Detective Rollins we'd stay here to talk to his men when they arrive."

Joe tossed Mike's registration card back in the glove compartment and grinned at Frank. "Well, you made the promise, so *you* can keep it. Tell the cops I was struck by a sudden, irresistible urge to go sightseeing on Esplanade Avenue."

Joe was already hopping out of Mike's car and heading off down the sidewalk. "Whatever," Frank called after him, laughing. "We're supposed to meet Nancy, Bess, and Shelley at Jackson Square at noon. Don't forget. And be careful, Joe."

"I can't believe we slept so late," Bess said, as she, Nancy, and Shelley walked through the French Quarter on their way to Thibaud's Creole Kitchen. "It's already after ten."

"We were up until after two helping Remy clean up at the restaurant," Shelley pointed out. "What I really can't believe is that he was up and out of the apartment before eight this morning to go back and finish up."

"We don't have to meet the Hardys for lunch until noon," Nancy said, glancing at her watch. "That gives us plenty of time to find out what Lisa Thibaud was up to yesterday and whether or not she had anything to do with sabotaging the Royal Creole."

Of course, they hadn't yet decided exactly how to go about that, thought Nancy. They would just have to play it by ear once they got there.

She breathed in the moist morning air as Shelley led the way around a corner onto Royal Street, stepping over the fat seams of moss in the brick sidewalk. Glancing ahead, Nancy saw a heavyset African-American woman wearing a flowing orange and purple dress. She was just stepping onto the sidewalk from a building with an awning over the entrance.

"Don't look now," Nancy said under her breath, "but isn't that Lisa Thibaud?"

Shelley stopped and followed Nancy's gaze, shading her eyes with her hand. Ms. Thibaud dropped her keys into an oversize woven bag slung over her shoulder, then started down Royal Street away from Nancy, Bess, and Shelley.

"That's her, all right," Shelley said. "I don't know where she's going, but at least it's not to the Royal Creole. That's back the other way."

"Still, I'd feel better if I knew what she was up

to," Nancy said. She raised an eyebrow at Bess and Shelley. "Do you two feel like following her?"

"We might as well," Bess answered. "I need to work off all the weight I put on eating Remy's yummy Creole specialties last night!"

Keeping a safe distance, they followed Lisa Thibaud half a dozen blocks to the end of Royal Street. As the heavyset woman turned right, Nancy noticed a streetcar slowing down.

"Oh, no!" Shelley exclaimed. "She's getting on the St. Charles Avenue streetcar. It goes straight through to the Garden District, but if we get on, too—"

"She might see us," Nancy said. "Maybe we can get a—" She did a double take as she spotted an empty taxi that was just passing by. "Taxi!" she cried, flagging it down. As the car stopped at the curb, Nancy grinned at Shelley and Bess. "Are we lucky or what?"

Shelley's eyes shimmered with excitement as she climbed into the taxi. "I never thought I'd say this, but . . . driver, follow that streetcar!"

Fifteen minutes later Lisa Thibaud got off the streetcar at the corner of Washington Avenue. Nancy, Bess, and Shelley quickly paid their driver, then followed Ms. Thibaud on foot.

The houses here were more stately than those in the French Quarter, Nancy saw. Most were hidden behind live oaks, Spanish moss, and colorful formal gardens. With so much to look at, Nancy had to force herself to keep her attention on the woman ahead of them.

Ms. Thibaud crossed the street and disappeared

inside a sprawling turquoise Victorian building, complete with balconies, columns, and a round corner turret.

"That's Commander's Palace, one of the best Creole restaurants in town," Shelley said, frowning. "What's she doing there?"

"There's one way to find out," Nancy said.

She, Bess, and Shelley crossed over to the restaurant and went inside. They were stopped at the maître d's station by a formally dressed young man. "I'm sorry, ladies," he said, "but proper attire is required here at Commander's Palace." He gave them a critical once-over, taking in their jeans and cotton shirts. "No blue jeans at any time, even for Sunday brunch."

He started to usher them outside, but Nancy held back just inside the door. "Could we make a reservation for another evening, say Thursday? We'll dress properly, we assure you."

"Wait here. I'll check," the maître d' said without enthusiasm.

Nancy had no idea whether they'd actually keep the reservation, but at least she had a chance to scan the restaurant. While the maître d' went back to his station and checked his book, she studied the restaurant from the entrance. There was a formal dining room, she saw, and a rear patio with fountains and lush tropical plants. It took Nancy only a moment to spot Ms. Thibaud. She was at a table on the patio, sitting with her back to them. When Nancy saw whom she was with, she drew in her breath.

"Oh, my gosh—that's Bill Jacobson!" Nancy said, her voice a shocked whisper.

"The food critic?" Bess asked.

Nancy nodded. Even though he was sitting down, there was no mistaking his barrel-chested build and shaggy beard. "Yesterday Lisa Thibaud *and* Bill Jacobson turned up unexpectedly at Remy's," she murmured. "Now here they are together."

"You don't think Bill Jacobson had anything to do with sabotaging the Royal Creole, do you?" Shelley asked, her eyes filled with worry. "I mean, why would he? It doesn't make sense."

"I know," Nancy admitted. Turning her attention back to Jacobson's table, she saw that Ms. Thibaud wasn't eating. She and the food critic spoke together for a few moments, and then she got up to leave. "Quick, let's get out of sight!" Nancy hissed to Shelley and Bess.

Whipping her head around, she saw a coat-check area in an alcove behind the maître d's station. The three of them ducked into the alcove, keeping their backs to the restaurant. Nancy waited until she heard the door open and close before she dared turn around again. Ms. Thibaud was gone, but the maître d' was looking at them as if they'd beamed down from another planet. He opened his mouth to say something, then snapped it shut again when a well-dressed elderly couple entered the restaurant.

"Shouldn't we keep following Ms. Thibaud?" Bess whispered as the maître d' left his station to seat the couple.

Nancy started toward the door, then changed her mind. "I want to see if I can find out what she and Bill Jacobson were up to," she told Shelley and Bess. "I'll meet you outside in a second."

She knew she had only a moment before the maître d' would return—no time for a subtle approach. Squaring her shoulders, Nancy walked through the restaurant, straight to Bill Jacobson's table. He was just putting his napkin on the table and signaling to the waiter for a check.

"You're Bill Jacobson, aren't you? The food critic?" Nancy asked. He frowned, but she didn't give him time to say anything. "I'm a big fan of your writing," she gushed. "And I really trust your opinion. I'll be in New Orleans for a few days, and I was wondering which restaurants you'd recommend."

Jacobson's eyes narrowed slightly. He stroked his thick beard as he scrutinized her. "Just read my column in the *Morning Sun.*"

"If you'd give me even one personal tip, it would mean so much," Nancy said, giving him her most charming smile. She lowered her voice before adding, "Didn't I just see you talking with the owner of Thibaud's Creole Kitchen? Should I go there while I'm in town?"

As soon as she mentioned Thibaud's Creole Kitchen, Jacobson's dark eyes flashed with anger. "I don't appreciate—" He broke off talking and signaled to someone behind Nancy. "This young woman is harassing me. It's an outrage!"

Uh-oh, Nancy thought. She turned around to find the maître d' glaring at her.

"I'm sorry, Mr. Jacobson. It won't happen again," the maître d' said. Taking Nancy's arm, he firmly ushered her outside. As she was leaving, she looked over her shoulder. Jacobson was staring at her, but there was an expression in his dark eyes she couldn't quite read.

Shelley and Bess hurried over to Nancy as soon as she was outside. "What happened?" Shelley asked.

"Not much," Nancy said. "Jacobson wouldn't mention a word of what he and Ms. Thibaud were talking about." She turned her head and looked up and down the street. "And now Ms. Thibaud is gone."

"We might as well head back to the French Quarter," Bess said. "We have to meet Frank and Joe at Jackson Square at noon."

"Let's take the St. Charles Avenue streetcar," Shelley said. "That way you'll get to see a little of the Garden District."

As they walked to St. Charles Avenue, Nancy was struck once again by the timeless grandeur of the Garden District homes. They were mansions, really, set behind graceful live oaks, willows, and wisteria. When they got to St. Charles Avenue, Nancy saw the olive green streetcar coming toward them beneath a canopy of oaks that arched above.

The streetcar was crowded, but Nancy managed to squeeze on behind Shelley and Bess. She felt herself getting wedged against the wall next to the door as other people pushed on. She twisted her head around until she saw Bess and Shelley, who were squeezed in next to the seats behind her.

I can hardly move, Nancy thought as the streetcar began to move, but at least I have a good view. When the door opened at the next station, she found herself staring at one of the most elaborate homes she'd ever seen. It was white, with Palladian windows, wrought-iron balconies, and a garden filled with more flowers and trees than she could begin to name. She leaned out, trying to get a better look at the front doors. It looked as if there was a phoenix carved into it, or a—

"Hey!" Nancy cried out as a hand shoved into the small of her back.

She threw her hands out, trying to grab onto the door, the guardrail . . . anything. But it was too late. She was already flying forward—right out of the streetcar!

Chapter

Nine

NANCY'S HEART leaped into her throat as she felt herself falling. The pavement seemed to rush toward her at lightning speed. She threw out her arms, then felt herself hit with a bone-crunching thud that sent shock waves through her.

In the split second before the streetcar door closed, she heard Bess calling, "Nancy!" Then the streetcar screeched its way farther down St. Charles Avenue.

"Ma'am! Are you all right?"

Nancy looked up to see a blond woman bending over her with a concerned look on her face.

"I, uh . . ." Nancy pushed herself up, feeling for cuts and bruises. Her palms were scraped, and her knees felt sore where they had hit, but she didn't think she had broken any bones. "I'm fine," she said.

"You've got to watch yourself on those old street-cars," the woman said, shaking her head. "It's easy to lose your step when it's crowded."

"Mmm," was all Nancy said aloud. To herself, she added, I wouldn't have lost my step if someone hadn't pushed me!

Frowning, she glanced quickly around. A hand-ful of people who'd gotten off the streetcar were walking away from the stop. Most of them tossed curious or concerned glances her way, but no one was acting suspiciously, nor did Nancy see anyone she recognized. Of course, whoever had pushed her could have scooted out of sight onto a side street or into one of the lush private homes. Or, he or she could still be on the streetcar—along with Bess and Shelley.

They'll probably get off at the next stop, Nancy reasoned. "I just hope they're all right—*and* that they saw what happened."

"I beg your pardon?" the blond woman asked.

It was only when Nancy saw the confused look on the woman's face that she realized she'd spoken aloud. "Oh—nothing. Thanks for your help," Nancy said. Then she set off down St. Charles Avenue.

She was still half a block away from the next streetcar stop when she spotted Bess and Shelley. As soon as they saw her, they ran toward her. "Nancy! Are you all right?" Shelley called, her brown eyes wide with worry.

"What happened?" Bess asked. "One minute I saw you squeezed in by the door, and the next you were gone. A guy on the streetcar said you fell. Are you okay?"

"I'm fine," Nancy said. "But I didn't fall. I was pushed. I guess you two didn't happen to see who did it, did you?"

"Pushed?" Shelley echoed. She and Bess looked at each other, and they both shook their heads.

"It was so crowded, I didn't see a thing," Bess said, looking upset. "Sorry."

Nancy ran a hand distractedly through her hair as she tried to think through the possibilities. "I didn't think Lisa Thibaud saw us at Commander's Palace. But if she did, she could have waited somewhere nearby and then followed us."

"The streetcar was so crowded, it's no wonder we didn't see her—or whoever it was," Shelley added.

"What about Bill Jacobson?" Bess asked.

Shelley drew in her breath in a sharp gasp. *"Please* don't tell me you think *he* did it," she said. "Bill Jacobson is a respected food critic. He could make or break the Royal Creole with his review. He just can't be involved in this."

"He probably isn't," Nancy said quickly. "I can't think of why he'd hurt us *or* the restaurant. And how could he have followed us so quickly? After all, he was still in Commander's Palace when we left. We surely would have spotted him if he was on the streetcar with us. But we have to consider every possibility."

The more Nancy thought over all that had happened, the more confused she became. "I wish I knew what he and Ms. Thibaud were talking about," she said. "And we still don't know whether Ms. Thibaud was the person who destroyed the cake or knocked out Remy."

"Well, we must be making *someone* nervous, or you wouldn't have been pushed from the streetcar just now, Nancy," Bess pointed out.

Nancy took a deep breath and let it out slowly. "Maybe Frank and Joe can help us reason it out while we're having lunch." She arched a brow and shot a rueful smile at Bess and Shelley. "But this time, let's skip the streetcar and take a taxi!"

Joe stood on the sidewalk and looked at 2316 Esplanade Avenue. The branches of a magnolia tree obscured much of the two-story Victorian house, but Joe saw porches on both floors, with doors to four apartments. Mike was in Apartment Three, he recalled. Apartments One and Two were on the ground floor, so Joe jogged up the stairs to the second-story porch.

"Locked," he muttered, after trying the door to Apartment Three. He stepped back and walked around the side of the house. At the far end of the balcony, he spotted a small window that was open a crack. Yes! He was in luck!

The magnolia provided good cover, but Joe quickly checked to make sure no one was around before he pushed the window wide open and looked inside. It was a bathroom, he saw. A razor, shaving cream, and a toothbrush were laying on the sink, and there were some towels in a crumpled pile next to a dirty pair of black jeans on the black-and-white tiled floor.

"This looks like the right place," Joe murmured. He scrambled through the window, then stood silently for a moment, listening. Not that he expected to find Mike, but maybe the guy had a roommate. Hearing nothing, Joe tiptoed to the door and looked out.

The bathroom was off a hallway. Directly across, Joe saw a messy bedroom with an unmade bed. To the left, the hall opened onto a living area, with a couch, chairs, and a TV. Playing cards and magazines spilled from Mike's coffee table onto the floor. A counter on one side of the room separated the kitchen area. Dirty dishes were piled in the sink, and a bowl on the counter held blackened fruit that looked as if it had been there for weeks.

What a slob, Joe thought. In the living room, he spotted a desk nearly buried under piles of papers as well as half-empty cups of coffee. It looked like as good a place as any to start his search.

Joe pushed some take-out menus to the side, then leafed through a pile of racing sheets. Mike had circled favorites on just about every sheet, and he'd scrawled bet figures in the margins.

Hmm, thought Joe, tapping the racing sheets. Faye had mentioned that Mike liked to live fast and dangerously. Apparently, she hadn't been kidding.

Joe pulled open the top desk drawer and rummaged around. "Pens, papers, matchbooks," he muttered. "Nothing much here." He was about to close the drawer, when his hand hit something stiff, wedged against the very back.

"What's this?" He gave a tug, then pulled out a thick envelope. He opened the flap and took out a wad of papers that were clipped together. "These are IOUs!" he said as he flipped through them. "Five thousand to a guy named Clyde Ribelow, fifteen hundred to someone called Chico. . . ."

He made a rough tally of the numbers, then let out a low whistle. Mike owed upward of twenty thousand dollars!

Neither Faye nor Hugh Gatlin wanted to believe a family friend like Mike would steal from them. But these gambling debts showed he had a motive, and Mike had acted suspiciously from the moment Joe and Frank met him. All Joe's instincts told him Mike had been mixed up in the theft from the *Delta Princess*. The problem was, he and Frank still had to prove it.

And they had to find out who had killed Mike.

Joe checked his watch. Twelve-thirty. He was already half an hour late to meet Frank and the others at Jackson Square, but he knew he wouldn't have a second chance to look around—not once the police showed up. He was about to replace the IOUs when he spotted two more items at the bottom of the envelope. One was a scrap of paper with a telephone number scribbled on it. The other was a business card from a place called Mama Gayle's Boat Rental.

"Boat rental, huh?" Joe said out loud.

J. J. Johnson had said that whoever ran past him on the *Delta Princess* the night of the theft took off in a motorboat. Joe wasn't sure how Mama Gayle's fit into things, but he and Frank would definitely have to check the place out. The company was located on Big Bayou Black, Joe saw, taking another look at the card. There were bayous all around New Orleans. He'd have to ask Faye how to get to that particular one.

Joe pulled a pen and a blank sheet of paper from Mike's desk, then wrote down both the address of Mama Gayle's and the telephone number from the other scrap of paper. He folded the sheet and put it in his pocket, then returned the IOUs, telephone number, and business card to their envelope.

He was shoving the envelope back into the desk drawer when Mike's front door rattled.

"You got the key we found on the body?" a voice spoke up outside the door. Then Joe heard the hiss of a police radio.

Joe jolted to attention. Before he could move, he heard the scrape of a key in the lock. The police were about to catch him red-handed!

Chapter

Ten

THANKS FOR COMING with me to Mike's apartment," Frank said to Nancy, Shelley, and Bess. "I don't know what held Joe up, but I want to make sure he's not in trouble."

"That's understandable, especially after what happened to Mike," Nancy told him.

When Frank had met them at Jackson Square, he'd told the girls about finding Mike's body at the Riverside construction site and about Joe's plan to search Mike's apartment. As the minutes ticked on and Joe still didn't show up at the square, they'd all gotten worried. Finally, they decided to drive Faye's car to Mike's apartment to find him. As they cruised north on Esplanade Avenue, Nancy called out the numbers of the houses they passed.

She broke off when she saw Number 2316—and the NOPD cruiser parked in front. "Uh-oh," she murmured. "Looks like the police are already here."

As soon as Frank stopped at the curb, they all piled out. Nancy's gaze flew to the two-story Victorian house. She could just make out the uniforms of two officers on the upper balcony, behind the leaves of a magnolia in full flower. It looked as if they were pushing open the front door of a second-floor apartment.

"Oh, no!" Bess gasped, turning to Frank. "I hope Joe's not still inside!"

"If he is, he's dead meat," Frank said. "We've got to—"

"Aieee!" Before he could finish his sentence, Bess let out a piercing scream and fell to the sidewalk. "Help!" she shrieked, clutching her ankle. "Someone help me!"

Bess sounded so convincing that Nancy thought she might really be hurt—until Bess winked at her. Then Bess twisted up her face into an expression of pure agony. "My ankle," she moaned. "I think it's broken!"

The two police officers had stepped away from the apartment door, Nancy saw, and were watching Bess from the railing.

"Officers!" Frank yelled. "We need assistance!"

Nancy held her breath, then let out a sigh of relief as the two officers came down the stairs and toward Bess. Moments later, she saw Joe rounding the corner of the balcony that ran along the second floor. He must have climbed out a window, she thought.

Frank had spotted Joe, too, and he and Nancy

exchanged glances of relief. Now all Joe had to do was make it back down to the street without being seen.

"What's the problem?" one of the officers asked Bess.

"Ooooh," Bess moaned again. "I tripped and twisted my ankle. I don't think I can walk."

While the two officers examined Bess's ankle, Nancy risked another glance at Mike's house. Joe was just stepping onto the downstairs porch.

"Your ankle doesn't look swollen," the second officer was saying. He rotated it gingerly. "Does that hurt?"

Moving quickly and silently, Joe dodged around the magnolia tree to the sidewalk, then walked casually up to them. "Hi, everyone. Fancy meeting you here," he said. "What's the matter, Bess?"

Seeing him, Bess sat up straighter and the grimace disappeared from her face. "I, uh, thought I hurt my ankle, but you know what? It feels much better already." She moved her foot back and forth, as if to prove her words, then gave the officers an apologetic smile. "Thanks for your help. Sorry to have bothered you."

"Glad to help, ma'am," one of them told her. "You're sure you're all right?"

Bess assured them she was. As the policemen headed back toward Mike's apartment, Shelley turned to Bess and whispered, "Talk about an Oscar-winning performance. You were great!"

"Thanks, Bess," Joe added, holding out a hand to help her to her feet.

"All in a day's work," Bess said, buffing her nails against her sleeve. "No autographs, please."

Nancy laughed. "What about you, Joe? Did you find anything?"

"I'll say," he answered. "I'll tell you guys about it at lunch. I'm starved!"

"I know the perfect place," Shelley said. "Sid-Mar's, out by Lake Pontchartrain. You can't beat it for crabs, catfish, and mudbugs."

"Mudbugs?" Bess echoed, grimacing. "Is that something you're supposed to *eat?*"

"Absolutely," Shelley said. "Mudbugs are what the locals call crawfish. Come on. You guys can see for yourselves how delicious they are."

Forty-five minutes later, Joe, Frank, Shelley, Nancy, and Bess were seated at a table on the restaurant's screened-in porch. The place was very informal, with scarred Formica tables and plain bottles of catsup and cajun hot sauce. Joe's mouth watered as platters of fried catfish, stuffed crabs, garlic bread, and boiled crawfish were brought to their table.

Shelley showed them how to eat the crawfish. Joe plucked one of the scarlet boiled crawfish from his plate, twisted off the head, and sucked the tender insides from the shell. "You were right, Shelley. These mudbugs *are* great," he said.

"I figured we could use some down-home N'Orleans cooking," she said with a smile, imitating the distinctive New Orleans accent. Soberly, she shook her head and looked around the table with wide eyes. "After what we've been through today—Nancy getting pushed off the streetcar, you two finding Mike dead . . ."

During the drive to the restaurant, Joe had told the others about finding the IOUs, the phone number, and the card from Mama Gayle's Boat Rental. Joe was glad for the chance to go over the different angles of the case. They didn't stop talking about it even as they ate.

"So," Nancy said, after taking a bite of stuffed crab, "Mike's gambling debts give him a motive for stealing from the *Delta Princess,* but you still need proof."

"And we still don't know who killed him," Frank pointed out. "If Mike *did* help steal the money from the riverboat, maybe his partner decided to keep all the money by getting rid of him permanently. Or his murder might not have anything to do with the stolen money. Maybe he just got into trouble with someone he owed money to."

Joe had been mulling over the same thoughts, again and again. There were still so many unanswered questions. "What about the black Jeep?" he asked. "We need to find out if any of our suspects in the riverboat theft drives one."

It wasn't until the words were out of his mouth that Joe remembered Shelley was married to one of the suspects. "It wasn't Remy!" Shelley said, her eyes flashing defiantly. "We don't even have a car."

Joe wasn't sure what to say. He didn't want to insult Shelley, but he wasn't totally convinced of Remy's innocence, either. "I found something in Mike's car earlier," he said. "A canvas bag . . ."

As he described it, Shelley, Nancy, and Bess exchanged sober glances. "That's Remy's," Bess said. "Someone took it from the restaurant last night after they knocked him out."

"But why would Mike have it?" Nancy wondered aloud. "Do you think he knocked out Remy and then tore the restaurant apart?"

"I don't know why he would," Frank said. "But Remy *was* on the *Delta Princess* the night the money was stolen. Now Mike is dead, and we find Remy's bag in his car. I'd like to talk to Remy and find out what he knows about all of this."

Shelley's expression had grown more and more troubled as she listened to the others talk. "He didn't take the money. He just wouldn't," she insisted. "Besides, he's already got so much to deal with, what with his sister's illness and someone trying to ruin the Royal Creole."

"Frank and Joe have to check out every possibility," Nancy said. "Maybe they could talk to Remy after the restaurant closes for the night, when things calm down."

Shelley still didn't seem happy about the idea, but she nodded her agreement. "Okay—if only to confirm Remy's innocence, once and for all."

"Thanks, Shelley," Joe said. He jumped to his feet and reached into his pocket for the information he had written down at Mike's apartment. "Right now, I'm going to check out the mystery number I found. I saw a pay phone inside when we first got here."

Heading inside Sid-Mar's, he found the pay

phone near the bathrooms, put in some change, and dialed the number.

"A-One Answering Service," a woman's voice answered. "How can I help you?"

Answering service, eh? Joe thought. Could Mike have used the service to reach his partner in the theft from the riverboat? "I'd, uh, like to leave a message for Paul Dupre," Joe said, taking a stab in the dark. "Or Danielle Dupre?"

After a short pause, the operator said, "I'm sorry, sir. I don't show anyone by those names registered with A-One."

"How about Remy Maspero?" Joe tried, but the answer was the same. Remy wasn't one of the people who used the service.

Of course, the Dupres or Remy could be using aliases, Joe thought. He decided to make one last try. "This is Mike Keyes," he lied. "I've called before to leave a message for . . ."

He was hoping the operator would fill in the name for him. But all she said was, "I'm not at liberty to reveal the names of our clients, sir. Do you want to leave a message or not?"

"I guess not," Joe said. He thanked the woman and hung up, then went back to his table and told the others what had happened.

"We still have other leads to follow," Frank said. "We need to check out Mama Gayle's Boat Rental. And I wouldn't mind paying another visit to Dupre's to see what they've got parked in that carriage house we saw out back."

"Big Bayou Black is pretty far out of town," Shelley said, "and since it's already past three now, you're better off doing that tomorrow. But we could go to Dupre's tonight. Even if you don't find a black Jeep, at least you'll get another taste of New Orleans jazz!"

After lunch, Frank and Joe dropped Shelley, Bess, and Nancy back at Shelley's apartment. Then they drove to a service station to have a mechanic examine the flat tire now in the trunk of Faye's car. They were assured that the tire could be repaired and were told to come back in a couple of hours.

With some time on their hands, the Hardys toured the Outer French Quarter, visiting the Mardi Gras Museum and then the New Orleans Voodoo Museum. "Just in case Angela Dixon tries to do anything to Remy, we'll be able to defend him," Joe said, chuckling.

"Not funny," Frank said as they walked along Royal Street and back to their car. "Voodoo is all too real in this city. I could almost believe in it myself."

As they passed St. Peter Street, they could hear the strains of Dixieland music coming from Preservation Hall jazz club. "I just can't get enough of this 'N'Orleans' music," Frank said as he slowed his steps. "This place must be a madhouse during Mardi Gras."

"Yeah, and we missed it by just a few weeks," Joe said. "But if we had come then, Faye would have been in school and you wouldn't have been able to spend so much time with her," he added in a joking tone.

"Enough," said Frank, playfully punching his brother in the arm. The two boys jogged the rest of the way back to the service station to pick up their car.

While Frank and Joe were touring the French Quarter, Nancy and Bess were relaxing at the Maspero apartment while Shelley worked on her paper for school. Nancy read a local guidebook while Bess catnapped.

"Do you two feel like taking a ride with me?" Shelley asked after a couple of hours. She stood up and stretched. "I need to look up a few things at the library at school. I'd rather get the work done now, during the school break when it's quiet," she said. "And it's keeping my mind occupied," she added.

"I think I'll stay here if that's okay," Bess said. "We've packed so much into two days, I'm pooped."

"I'd love to see your school," Nancy said. "The description in the guidebook makes it sound gorgeous. And if I'm reading this map correctly, I'll actually get to ride the St. Charles Avenue streetcar once and for all!"

The campus of Shelley's school was as beautiful as described. The original building, dating back to the nineteenth century, was a huge stone structure with arched windows and doors. The rest of the campus was true to the original buildings in spirit, except for the library, which was modern.

While Shelley used the computer center of the library to compile some statistics, Nancy strolled around the zoo at Audubon Park across the street from the school. Next, she walked over to the Camellia Grill, a charming restaurant she had read about in the guidebook, and where she and Shelley had agreed to meet. As she sat at the counter set with linen napkins, she amused herself by listening to the banter of the wait staff.

She was ordering a cup of coffee when she noticed a familiar figure appear from the kitchen area. The colorful dress unmistakably belonged to none other than Lisa Thibaud! Nancy hunched down at the counter as she watched Ms. Thibaud. The heavyset woman chatted and laughed briefly with one of the counterwomen and then made her way to the exit. "Catch you later," she called over her shoulder, nearly colliding with Shelley, who was just entering through the front door.

"Fancy meeting you here," she said before Shelley could get a word out. "If I didn't know better, I'd think you and your friend who thinks she's hiding over there were following me around." Her gaze took in Nancy. Then, with a toss of her head, she swept out of the restaurant.

"Did you just hear that?" Shelley said as she sat down at the counter next to Nancy.

"I think this whole restaurant just heard every word," Nancy said with a shudder. "Even though there are more fun things to do in this city, we're going to have to pay her a visit again tomorrow. We need to find out once and for all what she was doing in the bushes behind the Royal Creole."

Frank sat at a table at Dupre's and looked around the jazz club. It was just after eight, but the place was already packed. On stage, Danielle was singing. She was accompanied by J. J. Johnson, wearing dark glasses and a suit, as well as a bass player and a pianist, neither of whom Frank had seen before. Frank remembered J. J. mentioning that he and Danielle often played at the club on nights she wasn't performing on the *Delta Princess*. Apparently, this was one of those nights.

Nancy, Bess, Shelley, and Joe were lost among the crowd of people on the dance floor, but Frank had opted not to join them. He'd get his dancing time in after Faye arrived.

Just thinking about Faye made Frank's pulse quicken. He and Joe had left a message at the Gatlins' telling her where they'd be. For the dozenth time since he'd arrived, he looked toward the door, but he still didn't see her.

Oh, well, he thought. As long as Danielle was occupied and the club was in full swing, this might be a good time to sneak out back and check for that Jeep.

He carefully scanned the club, searching out Paul Dupre. He spotted the wiry man standing next to the entrance, greeting patrons. Good. He seemed busy, too.

Frank got up from the table and wound his way toward the end of the bar and the hallway leading to the rear of the club. He checked behind him before stepping over the Employees Only sign and walking to the French doors at the back.

So far, so good, he thought. If I can just get out back before—

"Excuse me!" a familiar deep voice spoke up behind Frank. "No one's allowed back there."

Frank froze, then turned slowly around. Paul

Dupre was standing a few feet behind him. When he saw Frank, the cool expression in the man's eyes hardened to a steely glare. "You're one of the guys who was here yesterday with Faye Gatlin," he said. It sounded more like an accusation than a simple statement. "What's going on?"

"I, uh . . ." Frank smiled, shooting Mr. Dupre what he hoped was an innocent-looking smile. "My friends and I came to hear some music, and I thought I'd step out for some fresh air, that's all."

"Can't you read?" Mr. Dupre gave him a dubious look, flicking a thumb at the Employees Only sign.

Frank pretended to look surprised. "Gee, I'm sorry. It's just that, well, this building is so amazing," he said, making up his story as he went along. "We don't have anything like it where I'm from. I couldn't resist taking a look around."

"We provide jazz here, not house tours," the club owner said curtly. "If you came here for the music, I suggest you go back into the club."

Taking Frank by the arm, he steered him back into the main room. Paul Dupre stationed himself at the end of the hallway, crossing his arms over his chest.

Brilliant move, Hardy, Frank told himself. There's no way I'll get out back now, not with Attila the Hun standing guard.

Frank headed toward the bar to get a soft drink. The band was just taking a break. Danielle was holding J. J.'s arm, steering him toward the bar, and Frank was giving his order to the bartender, when J. J.'s gravelly voice distracted him.

111

"I smelled it," the older man was saying. "I'd know that scent anywhere!" J. J. clamped his fingers around Danielle's arm and whipped his head from side to side. "I tell you, I smelled it!"

Hearing the word *scent,* Frank jolted to attention. He hurried over to J. J. "Hi, J. J. It's me, Frank Hardy."

"Thank goodness." The older man reached out a hand, groping until he felt Frank's arm. "That cologne I told you about—"

"The one you smelled on the person who took off from the *Delta Princess* right after the money was stolen?" Frank asked.

J. J. nodded. "I just caught a whiff of it. The thief could be right here in the club!"

Chapter

Eleven

WE NEED to act fast!" Frank cried.

He turned left and right, carefully sniffing the air. Sure enough, mixed in with the smoky odor of cigarettes was a hint of something musky and fruity. "I think I smell it, too!"

"You can't be serious," Danielle scoffed. "There must be a hundred people here. Who knows how many of them are wearing perfume or cologne. How can you pick out one particular smell?" She brushed her mahogany curls from her face and arched an eyebrow. But despite her derisive tone, Frank thought he noticed a nervous glimmer in her eyes.

"It's a pretty distinctive smell," he said. "I'm going to try to track it down."

"Count me in," J. J. said in his raspy voice.

Ignoring Danielle's scowl, Frank took J. J.'s arm,

and they headed into the crowd. "I don't smell whatever it was I smelled at the bar," Frank said. "I don't think anyone right around us is wearing the cologne."

"This way," J. J. said, pulling Frank toward the rear of the club.

Frank wasn't about to question the man. After all, he thought, someone who couldn't see was probably especially aware of his other senses. Also, J. J. had smelled it on the thief. He trusted J. J.'s nose a lot more than he trusted his own.

As they approached the rear hall, Frank noticed that Paul Dupre was watching them closely. Trying not to be obvious, Frank carefully sniffed the air, but he didn't smell the cologne.

"There *are* a lot of people here," he said, turning back to J. J. "It's not going to be easy to figure out—"

The door to the ladies' room swung open in front of them. Frank did a double take when he saw who came out. "Faye!" he said. "I didn't see you come in."

Her vivid green eyes lit up when she saw him. "Hi, Frank. Sorry it took me so long to—"

"That's it!" J. J. interrupted, gripping Frank's arm more tightly.

Frank didn't have to ask what J. J. was talking about. The smell of fruity, musky cologne was almost strong enough to knock him over.

And it was coming from Faye Gatlin.

"Faye?" Frank asked, staring at her in confusion. "Isn't that *men's* cologne you're wearing?"

"Tell me about it," Faye said, rolling her eyes. "I must reek of the stuff."

"You and whoever ran by me on the *Delta Princess* the other night," J. J. put in.

"You mean—" The playful glimmer disappeared from Faye's green eyes as she glanced back and forth between Frank and J. J. *"This* is the cologne you smelled, J. J.?"

"That's it," J. J. said with certainty.

Frank gave Faye a quizzical look. "I don't understand," he said. "How did *you* end up wearing it?"

"We got some samples at the store," she explained. "I accidentally spilled some on my arm when my boss asked me to smell it."

"It's lucky for us you did," Frank said. "At least now we can find out what it's called."

Faye waved her arm in front of Frank and J. J., and the fruity smell almost made Frank choke. "It's called Bayou Boss," she said. "It won't be on sale for a few weeks, but the producer sent advance samples to stores in the area."

"Hmm," Frank said. "If it's not even on sale yet, there can't be *that* many people who have it."

"Not more than a few hundred, anyway," J. J. said, laughing.

"At least it's a start," Frank said. "Faye, do you think your boss would talk to Joe and me? I know it's a long shot, but maybe he remembers showing the cologne to one of our suspects in the theft from the riverboat."

"It can't hurt to ask," Faye told him, giving a shrug. "I have to work all day tomorrow. Stop by the store anytime." Grinning up at him, she added, "Now, can we please stop talking about work? I thought I was coming here to have fun."

She looked at him with her liquid green eyes, and Frank felt a bolt of electricity shoot through him. "You're on," he said. "As soon as the music starts up again, let's dance!"

"Thanks for letting me come talk to Remy tonight," Joe said later that evening, as he, Shelley, Nancy and Bess entered the clapboard house where Shelley and Remy lived.

Shelley let out a sigh as she unlocked the front door and led the way to the upstairs apartment. "I just want to get it over with," she said.

"At least Frank and Faye agreed not to come along," Nancy put in. "It'll be easier on Remy if he doesn't have to deal with a whole panel giving him the third degree."

Joe hoped he'd have better luck here than he and Frank had had at Dupre's. Paul Dupre had not let them out of his sight the entire evening. Every time Frank or Joe tried to sneak to the back courtyard, Mr. Dupre had headed them off. Joe was more distrustful of the guy—and of Danielle—than ever. But he still had no idea whether or not there was a black Jeep parked in their carriage house. And so far, he and Frank hadn't found a single shred of evidence linking the Dupres to the theft from the riverboat.

Joe hung back while Shelley unlocked the apartment door and led the way inside. "Remy? We're back," she called softly. "How did everything go at the restaurant?"

Remy was sitting in the living room, wearing sweatpants and a T-shirt. When he saw Shelley, he flicked off the TV show he was watching and got to his feet. "Great," he said, smiling. "We were packed the whole night, and the waiters said everyone loved my cooking. *And* Mr. Legarde called to say he's going to lend me the money to get Delphine's medical treatment started. He wants to make sure . . ."

Remy's voice trailed off as he looked at Joe. He didn't say anything, but Joe saw the distrustful look in Remy's eyes.

"Sorry to stop by so late," Joe spoke up. "But some things have come up, and I need to talk to you."

"What kind of things?" Remy asked.

Joe decided he might as well be direct. "Someone killed Mike Keyes this morning."

The guarded look remained on Remy's face. "Sorry to hear it," he said, crossing his arms over his chest. "But what does that have to do with me?"

"Why don't we all sit down?" Shelley suggested. Joe didn't miss the nervous catch in her voice as they all sat down on the couch and chairs in the living room. He could see how much it bothered her that Remy was a suspect, but he couldn't just let the whole thing drop.

"Frank and I searched Mike's car this morning after we found his body," Joe explained. "We found a canvas bag from a convention the National Culinary Institute had in San Francisco last year."

"It sounds like it could be the same bag that was stolen from the kitchen at the Royal Creole last night, when you were knocked out," Nancy added.

Remy blinked and shot a confused glance at Joe. "What are y'all getting at? I only met Mike Keyes once, two nights ago on the *Delta Princess,* and it wasn't under the friendliest of circumstances," he said. "Why would he come all the way to my restaurant, knock me out, tear the place apart, and then take only a canvas bag?"

He seemed genuinely perplexed, but Joe wasn't about to let him off the hook so easily. "That bag happens to be the same one you were carrying on the *Delta Princess* just before half a million dollars was stolen from the riverboat safe," he pointed out. "Are you trying to tell me it's just a coincidence that the same bag was taken from your restaurant, then turned up later in Mike's car?"

"It wasn't the same one," Remy insisted. "For your information, I have two of those give-away bags."

"Yeah, right," Joe scoffed. He couldn't believe the guy would try to pass off such a flimsy lie.

Remy started up from the couch, his face red with anger, but Shelley pulled him back. "Calm down, Remy, please."

"I think what Joe is wondering," Bess said, "is if Mike *didn't* take the bag you had on the riverboat, then where is it?"

Remy took a deep breath and let it out, as if trying to control his temper. Without saying a word, he strode to the closet next to the front door and began rummaging around inside. When he straightened up a few moments later, he was holding a canvas bag with a chef's cap printed on it.

"'National Culinary Institute, San Francisco, June fourth through seventh,'" Nancy read. Raising an eyebrow at Joe, she said, "It's identical to the one you found, just as Remy said."

Remy shook his head in disdain. "Not that it's any of your business, but *this* is the bag I had with me on the *Delta Princess,*" he said. "After I lost so much money, I was so disgusted with myself that I just threw the bag into the back of the closet."

"Mind if I take a look inside?" Joe asked.

"If it'll get you and your brother off my back, go ahead," Remy told him.

It wasn't the most enthusiastic yes Joe had ever received, but he'd take what he could get. Remy handed Joe the bag. Joe opened it and looked inside.

"Doesn't look like anything much," Nancy murmured, looking over Joe's shoulder. "A newspaper, an apron—"

"I *am* a chef," Remy cut in. "Last time I checked, that wasn't a crime."

Joe decided to ignore the sarcasm in Remy's voice. As he pulled out the apron, an envelope fell from between the folds of fabric. "What about this?" he asked, holding it up.

Remy frowned at the envelope. "I didn't bring any mail with me to the riverboat casino," he said.

"It's blank. There's no name or address written on it," Nancy commented.

Remy grabbed the envelope from Joe, opened it, and pulled out a sheet of paper. After unfolding it, he stared at it blankly. "Huh?" was all he said. After a moment, he held out the paper to Joe.

The paper had one short notation printed on it: "BTech TKO by DeutInd TBA next week."

"Looks like some kind of code," Joe said, staring at the cryptic note. " 'BTech,' " he read, turning the name over in his mind. "Sounds like it might be an abbreviation of a company name."

"Definitely," Nancy said. She bent to look at the note, her brow furrowed in concentration. "So does this other word, 'DeutInd.' "

"Wait a sec. What are those names again?" Shelley asked. Nancy showed her the sheet of paper. Shelley stared at it intensely for a moment, then said, " 'BTech.' I bet that's BayouTech!"

"Randall Legarde's company?" Bess asked.

Shelley nodded, her eyes still on the note. "It's one of biggest companies in Louisiana. And 'Deut-Ind' might be Deutsche Industries, a huge German conglomerate. We've covered them in my international business class. They have subsidiaries all over the world."

"What about the rest of that mumbo jumbo?" Remy wanted to know.

Joe took another look at the note. "Maybe it's not so cryptic after all," he said slowly. " 'BTech TKO by DeutInd.' I bet anything 'TKO' stands for takeover, which means—"

"That Deutsche Industries may be about to take over BayouTech!" Nancy finished, her eyes lighting up.

"If we're right then it's major news," Shelley

breathed. She glanced at the others. "I can't believe I haven't heard about this in my class."

"I think I know why. Look at the rest of the note," Joe said. He pointed to the last three words: " 'TBA next week.' "

" 'TBA,' " Bess repeated. "To be announced?"

Nancy nodded excitedly. "I bet you're right! News of the takeover must be secret if it's not going to be made public until next week."

As Joe stared at the note, a niggling suspicion worked its way into the back of his mind. "You guys, this note is giving advance notice of the buyout," he said slowly.

"Wow," Shelley breathed, brushing a hand through her brown hair. "If a huge multinational like Deutsche Industries is buying out BayouTech, then BayouTech stock is bound to go sky high. Anyone who knows about the buyout ahead of time could buy BayouTech stock now, then make a killing when the stock increases in value."

"But that would be taking unfair advantage of privileged information," Bess said, looking uncertainly around the living room. "Isn't that illegal?"

"Absolutely. I hate to say it, but whoever wrote this could be involved in serious criminal activity," Joe said. "Insider trading."

Chapter

Twelve

"INSIDER TRADING?" Nancy echoed. That was a major crime.

"But how did *Remy* end up with a note about the takeover?" Shelley asked. "It doesn't make sense."

Nancy frowned, trying to reason the whole thing out. "It must have happened while you were on the *Delta Princess,* Remy," she said. "Somehow, the envelope ended up in your bag."

Glancing at Joe, Nancy saw the dubious expression on his face. He was probably wondering whether Remy could have had anything to do with the note, but she herself doubted it. Remy had seemed genuinely surprised to see the envelope. If he *was* involved in anything illegal, he never would have shown them the canvas bag, or the note, in the first place.

"The bag was on the floor next to me at the

blackjack table," Remy said, breaking into Nancy's thoughts. "But I still don't understand why anyone would put information about a secret buyout in it."

"Maybe it happened by mistake," Joe suggested. "I saw the security tape, and it was a pretty chaotic scene, especially when you were struggling with the blackjack dealer and Mike."

"So, the envelope could have fallen in by mistake," Bess said.

The theory made sense, Nancy realized. "Maybe it's not a coincidence that the sabotage at the restaurant started right *after* your night on the riverboat, Remy," she said. "Whoever dropped the envelope may have been trying to get it back."

"I left the gaming room pretty suddenly," Remy admitted. "If someone *did* drop the envelope in my bag by mistake, they wouldn't have had much time to notice it was missing, let alone get it back."

He frowned. "But how could the person know who I am? He'd have to know my name to find me at the restaurant."

"Mike knew your name," Joe said. "He said you told it to some of the people at the blackjack table. He heard about your restaurant from them, too."

Remy gave a slow nod. "That's right. And since you found my other bag from the National Culinary Institute in Mike's car . . ."

"Maybe *he* was the person who was delivering the note," Shelley finished.

"Or receiving it," Nancy said. "Afterward, he could have tracked down Remy at the Royal Creole, knocked him out, and taken the other bag, thinking it was the one with the envelope."

Bess held up a hand. "Wait a minute. I'm totally confused," she said. "Are you trying to say that Mike was involved in taking the money from the riverboat *and* passing information that could be used in insider trading?"

"We don't know for sure if he was mixed up in anything illegal," Joe said. "But you have to admit, clues do seem to point his way."

"We still don't know who wrote the note about the takeover," Nancy said, thinking aloud. "Or whom it was intended for."

"Mr. Legarde is the CEO of BayouTech," Shelley said. "If anyone knows about the takeover, he does."

"But the note doesn't implicate him in any way," Nancy pointed out. "Besides, he's already going to profit from the takeover by Deutsche Industries, since his company will be worth so much more."

"Mr. Legarde couldn't be involved," Remy said firmly. "He wasn't even on the *Delta Princess* the night I was."

That didn't mean he couldn't get someone else to pass along the information, Nancy thought. But she still couldn't think of any possible motive he might have.

"There *is* one other person I know of who works at BayouTech," Remy said slowly. "Angela Dixon."

"The girl who threatened Shelley outside the Voodoo Museum?" Bess asked.

When Shelley nodded, Nancy turned to Remy and asked, "Did you see her on the riverboat?"

"No," he answered.

Nancy sat back and thrummed her fingers against the couch arm. "Still, it can't hurt to check her out. Even if she's not involved, we might be able to find out more about the takeover—and any inside trading that's going on," she said.

"Um, aren't you forgetting something?" Bess asked, looking at Nancy and Shelley. "Angela Dixon hates you, Shelley, and she saw us all together. What if she recognizes us?"

Joe grinned and said, "She doesn't know me. Why don't I go to her office? If one of you can come with me to point her out, we can probably sneak into her office while she's on her lunch break. She'll never even know we were there."

"I'll come," Bess offered. "But what about your case? Don't you and Frank have plans to check out the boat rental place on Big Bayou Black?"

"I could go with Frank, if he needs company," Nancy offered. "We can all rendezvous later in the day. In the meantime, I think we should all keep quiet about this." She looked soberly around the living room. "If the wrong person finds out we're looking into the possibility of insider trading, we could all be in big trouble."

"I didn't realize Big Bayou Black was in the middle of Cajun country," Nancy said as she and Frank headed west of New Orleans in Faye's car on Monday morning.

Frank took his eyes off the road just long enough to glance at the live oak, willow, ash, and gum trees that forested the swampy low-lying land they were driving through. The road wound along next to sluggish dark bayous, and humid air blew in the open windows of the car. Just before he turned his attention back to the road, Frank spotted a heron wading in the water.

"It looks more like a wildlife preserve than a place where people live," he commented. "But Faye says Cajuns have been living here since the seventeen hundreds."

"There's the turnoff for Mama Gayle's Boat Rental," Nancy said, pointing at a sign up ahead.

Frank made the turn onto a small drive that wound around the water's edge. After about a mile, the drive ended in a muddy parking lot next to a swampy lake. A dock jutted out into the lake amid knobby cypress trunks. Next to the dock a low wooden shed stretched along the water's edge, surrounded by live oaks and cypress dripping with Spanish moss. The sliding door of the boathouse was wide open, and through it Frank could see rows of motorboats floating in the low water.

After parking, Frank and Nancy picked their way across the red-brown mud to a small wooden office near the dock. "Hello?" Frank called as he and Nancy stepped inside.

A tall, spindly woman in her thirties was standing behind the counter, flipping through a magazine. When she saw Frank and Nancy, a smile spread across her face. "Mornin', folks. I'm Mama Gayle. What can I do for you?" Her drawl was laced with the hint of a French accent.

Frank had already given some thought to their cover story. "We'd like to take a look at a boat a friend of ours rented here last Friday," he said. "Mike Keyes?"

"Keyes, eh?" Mama Gayle opened a ledger and ran her finger down a row of entries. "Sorry," she said. "Twelve boats were rented out on Friday, but none of them went to your friend. But we've got plenty of boats if you're interested in taking one out."

Frank frowned. "We need to see *that* boat," he said. "You see, our friend had my camera, and he forgot it on the boat."

"We inspect the boats after every use. No one found any camera," Mama Gayle said.

"Maybe it was overlooked?" Nancy suggested. "If we could just take a look in the boat. . . . We don't know exactly what it looks like, but our friend did tell us it had a motor that backfired."

Tapping a finger against the glossy pages of her magazine, Mama Gayle frowned thoughtfully. "We do have one outboard motor that backfires some," she said slowly. "It's on a little boat we call the *Blue Liner.*" She took another look at the ledger, then tapped an entry near the bottom of the page. "Here we go. On Friday, it was rented to a Mr. B. Smith."

Frank exchanged a quick look with Nancy. "Mike could have been using another name." To Mama Gayle he said, "He's a tall guy, well built, with brown hair and freckles."

"That's the fellow, all right. I remember 'cause it was slow when he showed up—around two in the afternoon," Mama Gayle drawled. She glanced at her ledger, then gave a nod. "Yup. Two-fifteen, according to this. Said he'd be fishing till after midnight and wanted to know how late he could return the boat."

Nancy raised her eyebrows, and Frank knew exactly what she was thinking. If Mike *had* been fishing, it was probably for half a million dollars— *not* for catfish at the bottom of the bayou.

"I told him he'd come to the right place," Mama Gayle went on. "I never can sleep at night, so we stay open till all hours. Everyone who wants to fish the bayous by night knows to come to Mama Gayle's. Of course, most of them are luckier than your friend."

"What do you mean?" Frank asked. "He didn't catch anything?"

"Not a single guppy," Mama Gayle answered.

Frank wasn't surprised. If Mike had used the boat to steal money from the *Delta Princess,* he wouldn't have had time to pretend to go fishing. Still, Mike couldn't have stolen the money on his own. He had remained on the riverboat while someone else made away with the money on the motorboat.

"Did our friend return the *Blue Liner* himself?" Frank asked.

Mama Gayle thought for a moment, then shook her head. "No, he didn't, now that you bring it up. It was another fellow brought it back."

"What did the person look like?" Nancy asked, an excited glimmer in her eyes. "Do you remember?"

"Can't say I ever got a good look at him," Mama

Gayle answered. "He was pretty well covered up. Dark hat, sunglasses, a black bag over his shoulder. It was funny, though." She shook her head, laughing under her breath. "Most of our customers come back reeking of fish, but this guy smelled like he'd been soaking in a bath filled with perfume."

Frank jolted to attention. "Perfume? Was it a fruity smell? Kind of musky?"

"I'd say so," Mama Gayle said. "Now, are y'all still interested in taking a look at the *Blue Liner?* Why don't you take her out for a tour of the bayous?"

Frank looked at Nancy, and they both nodded. "As long as we're here, we might as well," said Frank.

Mama Gayle took a key from a rack against the wall, then led the way outside to the boat shed. She opened a creaky door at one end, then went inside. As Frank and Nancy stepped in behind her, Frank saw that they were on an inside dock that ran along the rear wall of the shed. A dozen boats were tied to old wooden mooring posts, and opposite them a wide open doorway gave access to the lake. Briefly, Frank heard something rustling through the dense foliage that surrounded the lake. He listened, but he didn't hear it again. Must have been my imagination, he thought.

"Here's the *Blue Liner,*" Mama Gayle announced. She stopped next to a small motorboat with a bright aqua stripe running around its hull. As she unlocked the padlock from the chain connecting the boat to the dock, Frank hopped in and started the motor. As soon as the engine turned over, it let out a loud, belching backfire that echoed in the shed.

"Sounds like the boat we're looking for!" Nancy said, grinning.

"Don't see any camera," Mama Gayle said.

"That's okay," Frank told Mama Gayle. "We hadn't planned on taking a boat out, but I'd sure like to see the bayou." He looked up at Nancy. "How about you?"

"Sounds great," Nancy agreed.

Frank gave Mama Gayle a deposit, then quickly checked out the boat. An extra gas tank rested next to the rear seat, and a tarp was wadded up beneath the seat. A wooden pole stuck out from under it, stretching almost the length of the boat.

"Watch the shallows. They can take you by surprise," Mama Gayle told them. "If you need to, you can use that pole to help get out of tight spots."

A minute later Frank and Nancy were buzzing toward the murky waters of a bayou that snaked through the trees at the lake's edge. The moist air on Frank's arms felt so good that he didn't say anything at first. Upon reaching the bayou, he eased off the throttle and maneuvered the boat into the black, sluggish waters. The air buzzed with the sounds of birds, frogs, and bugs. Two egrets stood among the reeds next to a half-submerged cypress log, and thick Spanish moss hung from tree branches above.

"Wow," said Frank, taking it all in. "Faye told me the bayous were amazing. She was right."

Faye's name had automatically popped out of his

mouth, but seeing the sideways glance Nancy gave him, he felt oddly self-conscious. Shoving his free hand into his pocket, he watched a heron dart its head underwater, then pull out a fish.

"You and Faye have been spending a lot of time together, haven't you," Nancy said.

Frank felt weird talking to Nancy about another girl. After all, even though he and Nancy weren't dating, they always had had a special bond. But when Frank looked back at her, she flashed him a warm smile and added, "She seems really nice."

"She is," he said. "I don't know where it's all going, but—"

The boat lurched to a stop, and he and Nancy had to grab the sides to keep from losing their balance.

"Uh-oh," Nancy said, peering over the side of the *Blue Liner*. "Looks like we hit some of those shallows Mama Gayle warned us about."

While Nancy angled the motor up out of the water, Frank reached for the pole from the bottom of the boat. As he pulled it from beneath the tarp, a flickering movement caught his attention. A striped brown snake slithered from beneath the tarp. When Frank saw its splotchy brown coloring and the pitted indentations next to its eyes, he gasped.

"Nancy, watch out!" Frank shouted. "There's a water moccasin heading right for your feet!"

Chapter
Thirteen

NANCY WHIRLED AROUND in time to see the poisonous snake dart toward her feet.

"No!" she cried.

In a flash, she vaulted over the side of the motorboat, splashing into the bayou. Cold, dark water closed in around her, making her heart feel as if it were freezing up in her chest. As she thrashed her arms and legs around, trying to find her footing, she felt herself brush against slimy rotten vegetation.

"Ugh!" she cried, with a shiver. Swiping her soaked hair out of her face, she shot a panicked look at the boat. Where was that water moccasin?

Frank was poking at the bottom of the *Blue Liner* with the pole, his jaw tight with concentration. A second later, he used the pole to flip the writhing snake over the side of the boat. "It's out!"

"And so am I!" Nancy gasped. Frank had tossed the water moccasin over the opposite side of the boat from where she was, but she still didn't want to take any chances. "Help me back in—quick!"

She reached for the hand he held out and scrambled back into the boat. Moments later she was sitting, breathless, in a pool of swamp water. She was totally soaked, and bits of reeds and cypress bark stuck to her hair and clothes. The sour smell of the bayous clung to her.

"Th-thanks," she said. "That was a close call. If you hadn't seen that water moccasin—"

"Hey, no problem. I'm just glad the thing didn't bite you," he said. "Are you sure you're okay?"

"Fine," she assured him. She picked at the wet hem of her T-shirt and shot him a rueful smile. "But I don't think these clothes will ever be the same."

Frank stared out at the water. "What was that thing doing in our boat, anyway? I mean, I know there are poisonous snakes in the bayous, but—"

"You think this might not have happened by chance?" Nancy asked, blinking in surprise. "But how could anyone have planted the water moccasin? No one knows we're here except Joe, Bess, and Shelley."

"And J. J. Johnson." Frank's dark eyes flashed moodily as he took the pole and guided the motorboat to deeper water. "I called him before we left to see if he could come with us. I thought if we found the boat used in the theft, the sound of the motor might jog his memory and get him to remember more about that night."

"J. J.'s not a suspect, though," Nancy said.

"No, but Danielle is. So is her uncle Paul. And J. J. knows both of them. He could have mentioned our plans," Frank said. After lowering the outboard motor back into the water, he started it, then steered the boat back toward Mama Gayle's. "If either of them was lurking around here this morning, maybe Mama Gayle saw them. Let's go find out."

Mama Gayle came out to meet them while they were mooring the boat inside the boat shed. "Goodness!" she said, taking one look at Nancy. "What happened?"

When Frank and Nancy told her about the water moccasin, Mama Gayle frowned and shook her head. "It doesn't make sense," she told them. "Snakes usually keep away from the activity of the shed. It must be, oh, a year or more since I've seen one in here."

Nancy caught the grim look Frank shot her. Maybe the water moccasin *had* been planted. But how?

"Has anyone else been here this morning?" she asked Mama Gayle.

"Let's see. My husband took a family from Minnesota out on a boat tour of the bayous," Mama Gayle said. "But they left before eight and won't be back until after lunch. You two are the only other customers I've had."

"You haven't seen a girl?" Frank asked. "Pretty, with curly brown hair and high cheekbones? Or maybe a wiry man with short, reddish brown hair?" When Mama Gayle shook her head, he let out his breath in a disappointed rush.

Turning to Nancy, Frank said, "I'd still like to call J. J. and see if he told anyone about our coming here."

Nancy was still dripping wet, so she waited at the edge of the parking lot while Frank used the phone in Mama Gayle's office. When he emerged from the office a few minutes later, Nancy could tell by the sober expression in his eyes that he'd learned something. "What is it?" she asked.

"J. J. *did* tell someone else we were coming here," he said. "Danielle Dupre."

Frank left the car windows wide open as he drove through the French Quarter a few hours later. He'd just dropped off Nancy at the Masperos' apartment. Faye's car still smelled like swamp gas, but Frank had too much on his mind to do anything about it.

So, he thought, Danielle knew that Nancy and I were going to Mama Gayle's. Thinking back, he remembered that when he and Nancy had first gone inside the boat shed, he'd heard a noise in the woods outside. He'd dismissed it at the time, but now he wondered if Danielle could have parked somewhere near Mama Gayle's boat rental and then sneaked to the boathouse and planted the water moccasin in the boat.

Frank shook himself, turning his attention back to the traffic around him. He still had a few hours to kill before meeting Nancy, Bess, Shelley, Joe, and Faye for dinner. He wanted to update Hugh Gatlin on the case, but first he planned to talk to Faye's boss at the store where she worked.

Faye had told him that Michaud's was in Canal Place, a mall at the very foot of Canal Street, next to the Mississippi River. After finding a parking spot, Frank entered the shopping center, which had marble floors and a big landscaped atrium at the center of three tiers of stores. Frank found Michaud's on the second level.

"Over here, Frank!" he heard Faye call while he was scanning the counters of accessories and perfumes. Turning in the direction of her voice, he saw that she was standing behind a display of silk scarves, talking to a slender, well-dressed man with a closely trimmed beard.

Faye tapped the slender man on the arm as Frank went over to them. "This is my boss, Justin Lemoyne," she said. "Mr. Lemoyne, meet Frank Hardy, the guy I was telling you about."

"Faye says you're trying to find someone who wears the new Bayou Boss cologne," Mr. Lemoyne said, holding a hand out to Frank.

"That's right," Frank told him. "I was hoping you could tell me whom you've shown the cologne to so far. It's a long shot, but it might help us find the person who robbed Mr. Gatlin's riverboat."

Thinking, Mr. Lemoyne pressed his lips together and tapped his fingers against the glass counter of the display case. Finally, he said, "The samples arrived on Friday. I showed them to Cassandra Lewis, of course."

"She's in charge of the perfume counter," Faye put in. She pointed to a tall, striking woman at a nearby counter. Frank didn't recognize her from the security tape he'd seen, but he made a mental note of her name and face. "Anyone else?"

"Let's see. There are a few other salespeople in perfumes, and the customers we were waiting on at the time," Mr. Lemoyne said. "I'm sure I showed the Bayou Boss samples to them, too."

"Do you remember any names?" Frank asked.

Mr. Lemoyne thought for a moment, then shook his head. "We get so many tourists, their faces are just a blur to me. I'm afraid—" Suddenly he snapped his fingers. "There *was* one person I know, a local club owner. I've spent many evenings listening to jazz at his club."

"Jazz?" Frank jolted to attention and fixed Mr. Lemoyne with a probing gaze. "You don't mean Paul Dupre, do you?"

"He's the one," Mr. Lemoyne said.

"He was in here on Friday?" Frank asked.

"Yes. He was looking to buy some nice perfume for his niece," Mr. Lemoyne answered, "and I happened to show him a sample of Bayou Boss for himself. I remember thinking it odd that he'd spend money on an extravagant gift, since his club has had such money troubles these past few years."

It *was* odd, Frank reflected. Then again, if Paul had a plan to steal half a million dollars later that evening, maybe he'd decided to spend a little of the money in advance.

So far, the Dupres had managed to sidestep

every attempt Frank and Joe had made to investigate them. Somehow, he and Joe would have to make sure their next try was more successful.

"Is Angela Dixon *ever* going to take a lunch break?" Joe muttered.

For the past three hours, he and Bess had been sitting on a bench outside the sleek chrome-and-glass BayouTech office building, on Tchoupitoulas Street, near the river. It was already after two. He and Bess had gotten so hungry, they'd picked up sandwiches at a nearby deli and eaten them outside.

"What if she's eating at her desk?" Bess asked, peeking over the newspaper she was holding as a cover. "How will we get into her office?"

Joe shrugged. "We'll figure something out. If she doesn't leave the building in the next—"

"There she is!" Bess hissed, raising her newspaper to cover her face again. *"Please* don't look over here," she said under her breath.

A young woman with flaming red hair pulled back into a knot was just leaving the BayouTech building. She walked quickly down the street.

"She didn't even glance this way, Bess," Joe said. "Come on. Let's go in."

The lobby was ultramodern, with a bank of computer directories visitors could use to locate BayouTech personnel. Joe punched Angela's name into the keyboard, and a message flashed on the screen almost immediately.

"She's in room nine-fourteen," Joe said. He shot a sideways look at the security desk in a corner of the lobby. Seeing that a group of Japanese businessmen were talking to the guard, Joe took Bess's arm and led her quickly to the elevators.

"We have to act like we belong here," Joe said as they rode up to the ninth floor.

"Compared to my award-winning performance when I pretended to sprain my ankle, this will be a piece of cake," Bess replied. When the elevator doors opened at the ninth floor, Bess marched off as if she owned the place. Joe strode purposefully behind her as they swept past the receptionist.

The ninth floor held a central conference room with glazed glass panes. Joe could see the silhouettes of people through the glazed glass.

A carpeted hallway circled around to dozens of offices behind the conference room. Room 914 was one of the first offices they came to.

"This is the place," Bess whispered, nodding to a sign next to the door with Angela's name on it.

As soon as Joe and Bess had slipped inside, Joe closed the door and looked around. The office was little more than a small cubicle with a desk, filing cabinet, and shelves. A computer workstation angled off one side of the desk.

"A place as big as BayouTech must have a network linking individual computers to a company-wide net of information," he said. "That'll be our best bet for finding out anything about the buyout by Deutsche Industries."

"If you say so," Bess said, shrugging. "I'll see if I can find anything in these files."

While she went to the file cabinet, Joe sat in Angela's chair and booted up the computer. It whirred and beeped into action, revealing a menu of choices: "Accounting . . . Internal mail . . . Client database . . ."

For the next few minutes he clicked through a series of menus and lists of files. "Yes!" he whispered. "There's a whole subdirectory on Deutsche Industries!"

"Good." Bess left the file cabinet she was riffling through and came to stand behind him. "Anything interesting?"

"I'm not sure." One by one, Joe began accessing files and scanning the contents. "So far, the information is pretty basic," he told Bess. "Annual reports, records of computer technology Bayou-Tech sold to Deutsche Industries." He shot Bess an apologetic glance over his shoulder. "There are half a dozen more files. This could take a while."

Just then, he hit the key to call up a file called simply "DeutI." Angela's computer beeped, and a message flashed across the screen: "Protected File. Please Enter Password."

"Protected?" Bess echoed, looking at the screen. "What does that mean?"

"It means that the only people who can access this file must have a pretty high security clearance," Joe answered. "Whoever made this document wanted to make sure not just anyone could look at it. It could contain sensitive information."

Bess raised an eyebrow at Joe. "Such as information about Deutsche Industries buying Bayou-Tech?"

"Exactly." Joe felt a rush of adrenaline as he

stared at the screen again. "Now, if we can just figure out what the password is."

Just then the office door swung open. Joe froze when he saw Angela Dixon walk in holding a brown paper bag. When she saw Joe and Bess, she stopped short.

"Uh-oh," Bess murmured.

We're in for it, Joe thought. He flicked off the computer, jumped up, and flashed Angela a smile he hoped was reassuring. "We were just—"

"This is a private office," Angela cut in. She practically spat out the words. "What are you doing messing around with my computer—"

She broke off and stared at Bess. "Hey! I recognize you," she said, her eyes narrowing. "You were with Shelley Maspero the other day."

"Hi," Bess said, with a weak smile. She shot Joe a panicked glance and stammered, "M-my friend and I were, uh . . ." Her voice trailed off. There seemed no way out of this jam.

Before Joe could come up with an explanation, Angela stuck her head out the door and shouted, "Someone call security! There are intruders in my office!"

Chapter

Fourteen

WITHIN MOMENTS, men and women in business suits crowded around the doorway. Questions flew back and forth: "What's going on?" "Who broke in?" "Where's the guard!"

Great, thought Joe. Everyone is looking at us as if we belong in a maximum security prison!

"Joe, what are we going to do?" Bess whispered.

"I don't know, but—" Joe stopped talking as he saw a familiar figure entering the office. "Uh-oh," he said under his breath. "Don't look now, but Randall Legarde just got here."

The CEO of BayouTech was wearing a double-breasted gray suit and a look that was all business. A building security guard bustled into the office right behind him. "This had better be important. We're in the middle of a meeting," Mr. Legarde said to Angela.

"I caught these two—"Angela pointed at Joe and Bess—"messing around with my computer."

Joe cringed when he saw the deep frown on Mr. Legarde's face. We're in serious trouble now, he thought. Think fast, Hardy!

"Uh, hi, Mr. Legarde. Remember us? Joe Hardy and Bess Marvin. We had dinner with you at the Royal Creole on Saturday night," Joe said. He was babbling, doing anything to buy time while he tried to think of an explanation that would get him and Bess out of this situation.

A glimmer of recognition came into Mr. Legarde's eyes. "What are you doing here?" he asked, gesturing around Angela's office. "Bayou-Tech has nothing to do with the restaurant."

Joe thought fast. Maybe there was a way out of this mess after all. "Actually, the reason we're here *is* because of the restaurant," he said. "We've been helping Remy try to find out who's sabotaging the place. It turns out that Angela Dixon may have a motive for wanting to hurt Remy."

"She's never forgiven Remy for breaking up with her," Bess added, with a wide-eyed, innocent look. "She even threatened Remy's wife."

"What!" Angela burst out. She whirled to face Joe and planted her hands on her hips. "How dare you accuse me of something so outlandish!"

"Is this true?" Mr. Legarde asked. He fixed Angela with a stern look. "I won't have any of my employees interfering with the success of the Royal Creole."

Angela's face was bright red. She opened her

mouth as if to object, then clamped it shut again. "Of course not, Mr. Legarde" was all she said.

"As for you," Mr. Legarde went on, turning to Bess and Joe, "I appreciate what you're doing for Remy, but if I catch you sneaking around Bayou-Tech again, I'll call the police."

Joe wasn't about to argue with the guy. "Don't worry, we won't make the same mistake again, Mr. Legarde. Thanks for being so understanding," he said.

Grabbing Bess's arm, he pulled her toward the door. "Come on," he whispered. "Let's get out of here before Legarde changes his mind!"

Joe didn't dare look back. But as he and Bess angled through the doorway and into the hall, he could feel Angela looking daggers at them.

After Frank dropped Nancy off at Shelley's apartment, she had raced upstairs and jumped in the shower, hoping to rid herself of the swampy smell of Big Bayou Black.

Then she and Shelley had made a trip to Thibaud's Creole Kitchen, hoping to question Lisa Thibaud about her rendezvous with Bill Jacobson. When they arrived, they found the door locked, but Nancy had spotted Lisa Thibaud through the glass window separating the kitchen from the dining room. After she knocked, Nancy had been sure that Ms. Thibaud had seen them, but the woman hadn't acknowledged them or opened the door. Finally, they'd had no choice but to leave.

"There's nothing more we can do now," Nancy said. "We've got to meet Frank and Joe in a few hours and, believe it or not, I'd like to take another shower. We'll have to try to get to Ms. Thibaud again tomorrow morning."

Shelley sighed. "Even just seeing that woman again today was too soon for me," she said.

Joe stared out the wraparound windows of Hugh Gatlin's office. After dropping off Bess at Shelley's, Joe had returned to the Gatlins' just as Frank got back from Michaud's. Since they had a few hours before they were meeting the girls for dinner in the French Quarter, the Hardys had decided to bring Mr. Gatlin up to speed on their investigation.

"You say the woman at the boat rental remembers Mike taking out a boat with a backfiring engine Friday night?" Mr. Gatlin asked.

Frank nodded. "He was using an alias, but the description fits Mike. And the boat fits J. J.'s description of the boat the thief used to make his getaway."

"So, it looks as if Mike *was* involved in taking the money from the *Delta Princess,*" Mr. Gatlin said. "Detective Rollins hinted as much when he called yesterday with the news of Mike's death. Said his men had turned up some important clues at Mike's apartment that they'd be following up on." He frowned and slumped back against his chair. "I trusted Mike. If he'd just come to me, I would have lent him the money he needed for his debts. Now, I'm missing half a million dollars, and Mike is dead."

Joe couldn't help feeling bad for Mr. Gatlin. It was shocking enough that an old family friend like

Mike had betrayed his trust. On top of that, Mr. Gatlin seemed to take it as his personal responsibility that Mike had been murdered.

"Mike had to be working with a partner," Frank pointed out. "Mama Gayle remembers someone *else* bringing the boat back, someone who was wearing a cologne that sounds as if it was Bayou Boss. She couldn't describe the man, but I found out from Faye's manager that Paul Dupre tried out an advance sample of Bayou Boss at Michaud's Friday after—"

Frank broke off as he caught sight of someone in the parking lot. "There's Danielle," he said.

Joe immediately looked out the window and saw Danielle getting out of a green station wagon. Her mahogany curls cascaded over the shoulders of her evening dress. "She must be here to sing with the brass band on the evening cruise of the *Delta Princess.*" Shifting his attention to her car, he added, "Looks like she drives a station wagon, not a black Jeep."

"Which means she's not the person who nearly ran us down right before we found Mike's body," Frank said.

"What about Paul? How do we know *he* doesn't drive a Jeep?" Mr. Gatlin asked.

"Maybe Danielle can answer that question." Frank turned to Joe, a challenging look in his eyes. "What do you say? Should we have a talk with her?"

Joe was already out of his chair. "Definitely."

He and Frank flew down the stairs and out of the office, reaching the parking lot just as Danielle locked up the station wagon. Joe saw his brother pause, staring at the car tires. Frank followed his brother's gaze: Reddish brown mud was crusted all over the tires and had splashed onto the fenders.

"That looks a lot like the mud around Mama Gayle's," Frank said under his breath. A determined expression on his face, he strode the last few yards to Danielle. "Hi, Danielle. Been driving outside the city today?" he asked. "Maybe out to Cajun country?"

Danielle frowned when she saw Frank and Joe. She didn't answer at first, but finally she asked, "Isn't there any place in New Orleans a person can go *without* running into you two?"

"Afraid not," Joe said. Danielle hadn't answered Frank's question, he noticed. "Frank and Nancy were out that way today, too," he said. "They had a pretty interesting run-in with a water moccasin."

"Oh, yeah?" Danielle asked. Her face remained blank, but Joe thought he noticed a slight edginess in her voice. "Well, I'd love to stand around and chat," she added, "but some of us have to work for a living. If you'll excuse me . . ."

Without giving them a chance to ask about the black Jeep, she strode toward the pier where the *Delta Princess* was moored.

"Go ahead and run," Joe muttered, staring after her. "Sooner or later, we're going to catch up to you."

"There are Frank and Joe," Nancy said, as she, Shelley, and Bess walked into the Chartres Street Bistro on Monday evening.

She pointed toward the rear of the modern, informal restaurant, where the Hardys sat alone at a table for six. Abstract metal sculptures were scattered among the tables and near the bar, and photographs of New Orleans street scenes adorned the walls. As the three young women went over to the table, Frank smiled up at them.

"Hi, everyone. Hey, Nancy, why aren't you wearing that perfume you had on earlier?" he asked, a teasing glint in his eyes. "Eau de Swamp Gas, isn't that what it's called?"

"Don't remind me." She groaned. "I've taken two showers already this afternoon, and I could easily take another."

"Her clothes are still soaking in our tub," Shelley added, grinning at Nancy as they found seats around the table. *Without* any water moccasins."

Nancy shuddered every time she pictured the water moccasin darting for her feet. She shook off the thought and asked Frank, "Where's Faye?"

"Work," Frank answered. "The store is open late tonight. She said to go ahead and order without her."

The menu was filled with unusual dishes, Nancy saw, everything from pork pâté with pistachios to black bean cakes with crawfish salsa. She decided to try the house salad, followed by cedar plank trout with citrus horseradish.

After the waiter took their orders, Nancy filled Frank and Joe in on the frustrating visit to Thibaud's Creole Kitchen. She turned to Joe and said, "I heard you and Bess had a more exciting time at BayouTech this afternoon."

"That's for sure," Joe said. "It's a good thing Mr. Legarde is so concerned about the success of Remy's new restaurant. If we hadn't snowed him with that story about looking for the saboteur, you guys would have had to bail Bess and me out of jail. Angela was all set to call the cops after she saw us at her computer."

"If Angela has anything to do with leaking the information about the Deutsche Industries take-over of BayouTech, she'll work doubly hard to cover her tracks now," Nancy said, frowning.

"I was thinking, you guys should take a look at the security tape from the *Delta Princess,*" Frank suggested. "I mean, when Joe and I saw it, we weren't even considering a possible insider trading angle. Maybe you'll spot something we missed."

"It can't hurt to look," Nancy said. "You don't think Mr. Gatlin would mind?"

Frank and Joe both shook their heads. "We'll set it up with him," Joe said.

Nancy looked up as their waiter appeared with the appetizers. He placed Nancy's salad in front of her, and as she looked at the greens, she was surprised to see them artfully arranged with color-ful flowers.

"What beautiful flowers," Bess commented. "Are you supposed to *eat* those?"

"Absolutely," Shelley said with a laugh. "Edible flowers have been used in local restaurants for years now."

Nancy stabbed her fork into the salad, catching up a few blooms with the greens. Just as she popped the forkful into her mouth, she heard a horrified voice behind her say, "Oh, no!"

Before she could turn around, a hand reached in front of her and snatched her plate away. She turned to see Faye Gatlin holding the plate, her face white with fear. The next thing Nancy knew, Faye sent the plate flying to the floor. Lettuce leaves and ceramic pieces flew in all directions.

"What are you doing?" Nancy mumbled through a mouthful of salad.

"Those are oleander blossoms!" Faye cried. "If you swallow them, you'll die."

Chapter

Fifteen

In a single reflexive move, Frank jumped from his seat and bounded around the table to Nancy. "I think she already swallowed some!" he cried.

"If you swallow them, you'll die. . . ." Faye's words echoed inside his head, but he forced himself to push the thought aside. Please, he thought, don't let it be too late!

Joe, Shelley, Bess, and Faye all gathered around Nancy, too. "Call nine-one-one, quick!" Frank said. He was only vaguely aware of the buzz of shocked voices coming from the other tables. "We have to get her stomach pumped before the poison—"

Nancy bent over her plate in a convulsive motion that filled Frank with dread. In the next instant, she coughed out a mouthful of salad. Mixed among the half-chewed greens were two bright red blossoms.

"Nancy!" Bess cried. She held out her glass of water, and Nancy quickly swished her mouth out, spitting the last few shreds of salad into the glass.

"I'm—all right," Nancy choked out. "I didn't swallow anything."

"Thank goodness!" Bess breathed, her body going limp with relief.

"You're *sure* you didn't swallow anything?" Joe asked.

"Positive. I'm fine," Nancy insisted. But Frank noticed that the smile she turned to Faye was a little shaky. "Thanks, Faye. You saved my life."

Faye opened her mouth to say something but was interrupted by the maître d'. "What's the trouble?" he asked, frowning down at the shards of broken plate and scattered lettuce leaves. "If y'all aren't happy with the food, you could simply say so. There's no call for smashing plates."

"There is if that's what it takes to keep from being poisoned," Joe said hotly.

"Since when does the Chartres Street Bistro serve oleander flowers in their salads?" Faye asked angrily. She bent to the floor and plucked two red flowers from the wreckage. "Don't you know they're deadly?"

The maître d' took the flowers and stared at them in surprise. "They *are* oleanders," he said in a horrified whisper. "I don't understand. We would never include such things in our food, I assure you. How could this poison have gotten into the salad?"

"That's what we'd like to know," Frank said.

The maître d' quickly gestured to a busboy to sweep up the mess from the salad. With a flustered smile, he looked around the table and said, "Your dinner will be free of charge, of course. I'll speak to your waiter right away to find out what happened."

"I'd like to talk to him myself," Nancy said, getting to her feet.

"Me, too," Bess chimed in, staring at Nancy with concern.

Frank tagged along while the maître d' led them to the rear of the bistro. A hallway led past the kitchen to a courtyard, but the maître d' stopped at the waiters' station set into an alcove next to the kitchen doors. Their waiter, a tall, slender young man, was leaning over the counter, tallying a check.

"These people would like to speak with you, Patrick," the maître d' told the young man. "I'll talk to the kitchen staff myself," he added. "They're the ones who prepare the salads."

As the maître d' disappeared behind the swinging doors, Nancy and Frank told Patrick what had happened. "Oleanders!" Patrick exclaimed, his mouth falling open. "The salad has nasturtiums in it. The kitchen staff would never let oleander flowers anywhere near the food."

"Well, someone did," Bess pointed out. "The oleanders had to come from somewhere."

"What about back there?" Frank asked, nodding toward the courtyard. As he peered through the open door, he caught sight of some red flowering shrubs.

"There *are* oleander bushes in the courtyard," Patrick admitted, "but I don't see how any of the flowers could have gotten into your salad." He shot a sudden glance at the waiters' station. "Unless—"

"What?" Nancy urged. "Did something happen?"

"Well . . ." Patrick said slowly, a troubled look in his eyes, "as I was bringing out your appetizers, I *did* get distracted for a moment. I put the orders down here," he said as he tapped the waiters' station, "while I took care of a special request."

"Special request? Who made it?" Frank asked.

"One of New Orleans' most distinguished food critics," Patrick said. "Bill Jacobson."

Frank saw the grim looks that flashed between Nancy and Bess. "Didn't you two say Jacobson acted weird when you saw him at Commander's Palace yesterday?" he asked.

Nancy nodded. "Right before I was knocked off the St. Charles Avenue streetcar," she said.

"Mr. Jacobson was seated at one of our best tables, in the courtyard," Patrick explained. "He was on his way out when he stopped me. He started asking questions—about your table, as a matter of fact. He wanted to know what you were ordering, that kind of thing."

Something told Frank it wasn't simple chance that Jacobson had chosen *their* table to be curious about. "Didn't you think it was strange that he would ask about total strangers?" he asked the waiter.

Patrick shrugged. "When you work at a restaurant, the first thing you learn is *never* to question what Bill Jacobson says or does," he said. "I guess being the most respected food critic in New Orleans entitles him to be quirky."

Quirky is one thing, thought Frank. Deadly is another.

"You didn't happen to leave Jacobson alone with our appetizers, did you?" Nancy asked Patrick.

"I had to," Patrick said. "He asked me to get him a seltzer with a twist of lemon from the bar. Like I said, when Mr. Jacobson asks for something, you don't make him wait. It took only a minute."

Just enough time for him to get some oleander flowers from the courtyard and plant them in Nancy's salad, Frank thought.

"The funny thing was," Patrick went on, "when I got back with his drink, he said he'd changed his mind. Said he wasn't thirsty after all. Then he left. It couldn't have been more than a few minutes ago."

"Oh, yeah?" Nancy glanced toward the exit, her blue eyes gleaming. She quickly thanked Patrick, then pulled Frank and Bess away from the waiters' station. "Bill Jacobson could be long gone, but if he's still in sight, I want to follow him."

"I'm coming with you," Bess insisted.

"I'll stay behind and let everyone else know what's going on," Frank offered. "Good luck!"

Nancy felt adrenaline pumping through her as she and Bess hurried from the Chartres Street Bistro. Up and down Chartres Street tourists were ambling along, taking in the French Quarter or reading menus posted outside other restaurants. Nancy craned her neck, trying to get a glimpse of Bill Jacobson's stocky build and shaggy beard.

"Do you see him?" Bess asked, stopping on the sidewalk next to her.

Nancy shook her head, her gaze still playing over the crowd. "Not yet. It's pretty crowded. Wait a sec!" She grabbed Bess's arm and pointed ahead. "That bearded man up there, just crossing the street . . ."

"It's him!" Bess cried. "It looks like he's turning. We'd better catch up to him fast!"

They were still half a block away when Bill Jacobson disappeared around the corner onto Canal Street. Nancy and Bess raced after him, dodging tourists. Nancy kept her eyes glued to the spot where she'd last seen him. When they finally got to the corner, she whipped her head around and— "Yes!" she said breathlessly.

Jacobson was walking down Canal Street, heading south. He was moving at a leisurely pace, a leather briefcase in one hand. He didn't appear to have any idea he was being followed.

"Where's he going?" Bess wondered aloud, as she and Nancy followed, keeping half a block behind.

"I guess we'll find out," Nancy said.

The neighborhood Jacobson was heading into was a business district, Nancy saw. Restaurants and boutiques gave way to office buildings. After about ten minutes, Jacobson stopped in front of a large brick building. Nancy and Bess held back, watching him from the other side of the street.

"That's the *New Orleans Morning Sun* office," Nancy whispered, peering at a metal plaque next to the entrance. "It's kind of late, but newspaper people do keep pretty unconventional hours."

Instead of going inside, Jacobson ducked into the arched gallery that ran along the front of the *Morning Sun* building. Nancy saw him reach into his briefcase. He pulled out a cellular phone and dialed a number.

"I wonder why he's making a call from *outside* the building?" Bess asked. "You'd think the guy would have his own desk and phone right inside. Why bother to use a cell phone from out here?"

"Maybe because he's got something to hide," Nancy said, keeping her eyes on Jacobson. "Stay here. I'm going to try to get closer so I can hear what he's saying."

Jacobson was standing with his back to them in the shadows of the arcade, next to one of the brick arches. Nancy slipped quietly across the street. As she stepped into the shadow of the archway directly to Jacobson's left, she heard his voice.

"Be sure to give Mr. Redgale the message," he was saying. "It's very important. . . . Yes, thank you." Then Nancy heard a faint bleep as Bill Jacobson switched off the cellular phone.

Nancy stifled the groan that rose in her throat. If only she'd gotten there thirty seconds sooner!

Jacobson's shoes scraped against the uneven cobbles inside the gallery, startling Nancy from her thoughts. She quickly flattened herself against the archway. *Please* don't see me, she begged silently.

She heard his footsteps growing fainter. Relieved that he was walking in the opposite direction from her, Nancy risked a glance into the gallery. She saw Jacobson head for the rotating doors of the *Morning Sun* building. As he moved into the brightly lit area outside the doors, Nancy caught sight of a red blotch on the back of his sleeve.

It was a crushed oleander blossom.

Chapter

Sixteen

Nancy Drew in her breath sharply. She didn't think it was a coincidence that Jacobson was trailing oleanders just minutes after someone had tried to poison her with the same flowers.

But why would a food critic attack her? Was it possible that he was involved in sabotaging the Royal Creole? But why?

Nancy was more determined than ever to find out what Jacobson was up to. Outside the entrance, Bill Jacobson was just folding shut his cellular phone. Without looking, he dropped the phone into his briefcase, which he was holding with his other hand. But instead of falling inside the case, the phone teetered over the edge. As Jacobson opened the door, a man coming out bumped into him slightly. The phone fell to the ground. Jacobson glared at the man, then disappeared through the door.

Check it out, Nancy thought, blinking in surprise. Jacobson hadn't even realized he'd dropped his phone!

"So much the better for me," Nancy murmured. She jumped forward and grabbed the phone, then ran back across the street to where Bess was waiting.

Questions tumbled out of Bess's mouth. "What are you doing with Jacobson's phone? Did you hear anything he said?"

"He dropped it. I didn't hear everything he said, but I think I might have a way of finding out." Nancy turned on the phone, then hit the code to automatically redial the last number called. "Come on," she urged as she listened to the electronic bleeps. Moments later a pleasant man's voice said, "A-One Answering Service. How can I help you?"

Nancy blinked in surprise. A-1 was the same answering service Joe had called, using the number he'd found in Mike Keyes's apartment! Joe hadn't been able to get any information about who used the service, but maybe she'd have better luck.

"Hello? Is anyone there?" the operator's annoyed voice broke into Nancy's thoughts.

"Yes! Um, this is Mr. Jacobson's secretary," Nancy fibbed. "He just called to leave a message for Mr. Redgale," she said, recalling the name she'd overheard. "He's afraid he may have left out some important information. Would you mind reading the message back to me, so I can double check?"

There was a short silence, and Nancy heard the

rustling of papers over the line. She held her breath. Please don't give me a hard time, she prayed.

"Let's see . . . here it is," the operator finally said. "Mr. Jacobson will meet Mr. Redgale tomorrow night at ten o'clock, at Old St. Louis Cemetery Number One. That's all I have, ma'am. Was there anything Mr. Jacobson wanted to add?"

Nancy mentally filed away the information. "No, that's everything," she told the operator. "I guess Mr. Jacobson was worried over nothing. Thanks very much for your help."

"We did it!" Nancy crowed as she turned off the cellular phone. "I found out who Mr. Jacobson was talking to! The same answering service that Mike Keyes had a number for. Mr. Jacobson is going to meet someone named Mr. Redgale at a cemetery tomorrow night at ten. Old St. Louis Cemetery Number One."

"A cemetery? At night?" Bess echoed, raising a brow at Nancy. "Doesn't that sound suspicious?"

"It certainly does," Nancy agreed. "I don't know who this guy Redgale is or what he and Jacobson are up to. But when they meet tomorrow night, I'm going to be there."

"Mmm. Coffee and beignets from the Café du Monde," Bess said on Tuesday morning as she, Shelley, and Nancy walked through the French Quarter on their way to the Royal Creole. Bess grinned, holding up a paper bag containing four take-out cups of chicory coffee. "This is my idea of the perfect breakfast."

"Mine, too," Shelley agreed. She smiled at Nancy, who was carrying a dozen beignets in another paper bag. "And Remy's. I can't wait to see him. It seems like years since I've spent any time with him."

"That's not surprising," Nancy put in. "We were asleep when he got back from the Royal Creole last night. By the time we woke up this morning, he was already up and gone."

"Remy likes to get to the fish and produce markets early, so he can choose the freshest goods himself," Shelley explained. "Since we can't afford a car yet, either Jorge or Emil, the sous chefs, drive him."

When they got to the restaurant, the kitchen counters were piled with fruits, vegetables, and greens. Remy was just lugging a crateful of shrimp packed in ice into his walk-in refrigerator. "Mmm, is that chicory coffee?" he asked, wiping his hands on his apron as he emerged from the refrigerator.

"And beignets." Shelley gave him a kiss, then pushed aside a pile of okra to make room for the coffee and doughnuts. "We figured you could use a break while we fill you in on all that's been happening."

While they ate, Nancy, Bess, and Shelley told Remy about the oleander flowers that had been planted in Nancy's salad and about what had happened when they followed Bill Jacobson afterward.

"You think Jacobson tried to hurt you?" Remy asked, his mouth dropping open. "But why would he?"

"I don't know, but I've been attacked twice now, and Jacobson was on the scene both times," Nancy said. "He did show up here right after we found you knocked out and the kitchen wrecked the other night. We have to consider that he may have been involved."

"Besides, if he's making a rendezvous in a cemetery in the middle of the night, he must be up to *something,*" Bess added.

Remy ran a hand distractedly through his thick dark hair. "But Lisa Thibaud was here Saturday evening, too. Shouldn't you be investigating her instead of bothering a food critic whose review could be critical to the success of my restaurant?"

"Nancy hasn't ruled out Lisa Thibaud as a suspect," Shelley put in quickly. "In fact, we went over to her restaurant yesterday to question her, with no luck."

"Lisa Thibaud was with Bill Jacobson at Commander's Palace," Nancy said. "We're going to make another attempt to get into her restaurant and see if we can find anything linking her to the sabotage."

Everyone was silent for a moment, considering all the angles. "And what about the note we found in your bag, Remy—the note about the takeover?" Nancy went on. "If you ask me, that's still the strongest motive we've found for the sabotage. Whoever wrote the note broke in here and trashed the place, hoping to get the note back before anyone else could find it."

"That's true. But the bag was found in Mike

Keyes's car, not Bill Jacobson's," Remy pointed out.

"I'm not sure what to make of that," Nancy admitted. "Frank and Joe arranged for us to look at the security tape from the *Delta Princess* later this morning. Maybe we'll know more after we see it."

"Such as whether Mike, or Jacobson, or Angela Dixon had anything to do with passing that note," Shelley said, "and leaking advance word of the BayouTech takeover."

Just then there was a knock at the half-open kitchen door, and someone called, "Hello?"

Nancy turned to see Randall Legarde standing there in an immaculate cream-colored suit. "Hi, Mr. Legarde," Remy said, looking surprised. "I wasn't expecting to see you here this morning."

Neither was I, thought Nancy, groaning inwardly. She hoped he hadn't overheard what Shelley had said about the BayouTech takeover. But if he had, he showed no indication of it.

"I thought I'd stop by on the spur of the moment," Mr. Legarde said. "I've been worried about the recent acts of sabotage. Is everything all right?"

"There haven't been any more attacks, thank goodness," Shelley said, smiling at him.

"Glad to hear it." As Mr. Legarde stepped into the kitchen, his alert gaze swept over the room. Nancy saw his eyes narrow as they fell on Bess. Obviously he recognized her from the BayouTech office, but he didn't say anything about it.

"Well, I won't keep you, Remy," he went on, glancing at the produce piled high on the counters. "I see you have plenty of work to do."

Nancy didn't miss the way Mr. Legarde frowned at her, Shelley, and Bess. Obviously, he didn't want *them* to distract Remy from his work, either.

"We, uh, have to be going, too," Shelley said quickly, taking the hint. "We'll call you later, Remy."

"Dupre's looks quiet," Frank said as he and Joe stopped on Bourbon Street, just across from the jazz club. "In fact, all of Bourbon Street is pretty tame this early in the day."

Joe couldn't argue with that. The neon signs had been turned off, and the late-night partyers were gone. It was exactly what they'd been hoping for. "It's still before nine," he said, checking his watch. "If Danielle and her uncle are sleeping in, we can make it in and out of their carriage house without them knowing we were there."

He and Frank followed the gravel drive around the side of the jazz club to the carriage house behind. Two wide wooden doors looked as if they swung open to allow cars to come and go, but Joe didn't dare risk making noise by opening them.

"Over here," Frank called softly from the side of the carriage house. "There's a side entrance."

Joe jogged around to the side of the carriage house and found his brother next to a wooden door. Frank was standing on tiptoe, feeling around the ledge above the door. "There might be a key around here somewhere. . . . Aha!" He pulled down a weathered-looking brass key and held it up with a triumphant grin.

Seconds later they were inside the carriage

house. Joe paused inside the door, blinking until his eyes adjusted to the half-light. Looking around, he saw that half the space was taken up by the green station wagon Danielle had driven to the *Delta Princess* the day before. The other half was filled with broken tables and bar stools, rusted iron grillwork, paint cans, old fans, and sagging, dust-covered boxes.

"No Jeep," Joe said, frowning.

"So maybe it wasn't Danielle or Mr. Dupre who almost ran us down before we found Mike's body," Frank said. "But they could still have been involved in the theft from the riverboat casino. Mama Gayle told Nancy and me the person who returned the boat wore a dark hat and glasses, and carried a dark bag. If we find that stuff here—"

"We'll have found Mike's accomplice," Joe finished.

While Frank headed toward the station wagon, Joe walked slowly to the other side of the garage and began poking among the cardboard boxes. "These look as if they haven't been touched in centuries," he muttered, brushing the thick dust from his hands. "There's no way anything's been put in them lately."

He peered underneath the old tables and chairs, but he didn't see anything unusual. He was about to give up, when he spotted something stuffed behind some boards leaning against the carriage house wall. He reached behind the boards and pulled out a black canvas shoulder bag. When he lifted the flap, he saw a dark baseball cap and sunglasses inside. They all smelled vaguely of fruity, musky cologne.

"Hey, Frank!" Joe called softly. When Frank's head poked out the driver's-side window of the station wagon, Joe held up the bag, grinning. "It smells like cologne, too."

Frank scrambled out of the station wagon, took the bag from Joe, and held it up to his nose. "That's Bayou Boss, all right." He frowned as he looked inside. "Sunglasses, baseball cap—the only thing I *don't* see is a half-million dollars."

Suddenly Frank cocked his head to one side. "Hear that?" he whispered.

Joe heard footsteps on the gravel a split second before the carriage house door swung open. He dropped to a crouch, ready to dive behind the station wagon, but it was already too late. Danielle stood in the open doorway, bathed in the low-slanting beams of morning sunlight.

And she was glaring right at Frank and Joe.

"What are you two doing in here?" she demanded. "Trespassing is a crime, you know."

"So is stealing half a million dollars," Joe shot back.

"What!" She looked back and forth between Frank and Joe. "You think *I*— That's outrageous!"

"You can cut the self-righteous act, Danielle," Frank said. "We've already tracked down the boat the thief used to make the getaway. The woman who runs the boat rental place said the motorboat was returned by someone carrying a dark bag and wearing sunglasses and a black baseball cap." He held up the glasses and cap, and tossed the black canvas bag to Danielle. "They were exactly like these, which we just found right here in your carriage house."

"The woman also remembered that the man smelled of cologne," Joe went on. "It was an unusual scent—strong, fruity, musky—the same cologne J. J. Johnson smelled on the thief. We happen to know your uncle tried a new cologne, Bayou Boss, at Michaud's Department Store a few hours before the money was stolen." He crossed his arms over his chest, fixing Danielle with a probing stare. "Your uncle doesn't exactly make a secret of the fact that he blames Hugh Gatlin for the money troubles he's had since Mr. Gatlin pulled out of the jazz club. *Try* to tell me he wasn't in on the theft."

For once the sarcastic defiance left Danielle's face. She glanced at the black bag, then at the Hardys, and a look of desperation crossed her face. But still she said nothing.

"Look, Danielle," said Frank, "you're going to be in big trouble with the police unless—"

"I didn't do anything!" she burst out. She took a few deep breaths, as if trying to gain control of herself. When she spoke again, her voice was barely above a whisper: "But there *has* been some weird stuff going on the past few weeks."

Joe blinked in surprise. They'd finally cracked Danielle's defensive armor. "Can you be a little more specific?" he asked.

"Well . . ." Danielle took a deep breath, then said, "When I got back from work on the *Delta*

Princess Friday night, Uncle Paul wasn't at the club. That's pretty unusual. Ever since his partner took off with the club's money, he likes to keep a close eye on things here."

"When did he come back?" Frank asked.

"It was after three," she answered. "He smelled of cologne, but I didn't think anything about it until you two showed up the next day and mentioned it. When I asked Uncle Paul, he said he hadn't worn cologne at all, that what I'd smelled was a *perfume* he'd bought—for me."

Looking back and forth between Frank and Joe, she gave them an embarrassed smile. "It was such a nice present, and I guess I didn't want to believe he could be mixed up in anything illegal. I convinced myself that I had been mistaken about the cologne."

Danielle sniffed the bag in her hands, then frowned. "But this is the same cologne I smelled on Uncle Paul Friday night. The perfume he gave me is totally different."

Danielle was acting sincere, but Joe still had some doubts about whether she herself was involved. "Mike came by here the day after the theft. He was willing to brain me with a piece of metal railing in order not to be seen," Joe said. "That night, I saw you talking to him on the deck outside the gaming room of the *Delta Princess,* but you lied and said you hadn't seen him. If you weren't in on something suspicious, then why did you lie to me?"

"And what was Mike doing here in the first place?" Frank added.

"I don't know why he was here," Danielle said, with a helpless shrug. "I always knew Mike was trouble—into gambling and stuff. When I realized he'd been here, I was afraid he was trying to get Uncle Paul involved in something shady. That's why I followed him on the riverboat—to tell him to leave my uncle alone."

Looking out the open carriage house door, Joe saw the French doors at the back of Dupre's push open. "Danielle?" Paul called, sticking his head out. "Are you out here?"

As Joe watched, Danielle turned, and Joe saw her uncle look at the black canvas bag in her hand. As he walked toward her, Dupre seemed to notice Frank and Joe, standing inside the carriage house, for the first time. His whole face changed. His beady eyes flickered suspiciously over the brothers.

"What's going on?" Dupre asked, walking into the carriage house.

Joe wasn't about to let Paul Dupre slip away from them this time. "Come off it, Dupre," he said. "We know you're the one who took the money from the *Delta Princess*. We found the bag you used to carry the money, and the glasses and cap you wore."

"Nice theory, but you're forgetting something, aren't you?" Paul asked. "If I stole that money, then where is it?"

The look on his face was so smug that Joe wanted to slug him. Joe took a step forward, his hands clenched into fists, but Frank grabbed his arm.

"The police will be all over this place as soon as Joe and I show them this bag. And I'm sure Mama

Gayle won't have any trouble identifying you once she sees you in these," Frank said, holding up the black cap and sunglasses. "Why don't you save us all a lot of time and effort and simply tell us where the money's hidden?"

"Y'all are way off base," Paul scoffed. But his eyes flickered nervously toward the back of the carriage house. Turning around, Joe quickly scanned the items piled against the rear wall. There were some old stools, a table with an old ceiling fan lying on it . . .

"Hey!" Joe's gaze moved back to the fan. Unlike most of the other things, it didn't have a thick coating of dust on it. "Isn't that the fan you just replaced in your club?" he asked, thinking out loud.

As soon as he saw the panicked expression on Paul's face, Joe knew he was onto something. He raced over to the fan, with Frank right behind him. Six fan blades stretched out from a brass bulb at the center of the fan.

"There must be an opening where the fan attaches to the ceiling," Frank said, "to hook it up to the electrical wiring."

He and Joe turned the fan over—and Joe let out a low whistle. There, wedged inside the metal cavity were thick wads of hundred-dollar bills!

"Bingo," Frank said, his eyes fixed on the cash.

A scuffling sound behind them reminded Joe that Paul and Danielle Dupre were still there. He turned around, then gasped when he saw Dupre dart toward the cardboard boxes lining the carriage house wall. With a wide sweep of his arm, the man sent a huge pile of boxes crashing toward Frank and Joe. Then he spun around and raced from the carriage house.

Joe grimaced as one of the heavy boxes slammed into his hip, but he kept his eyes locked on Dupre. "Frank! He's getting away!"

Chapter

Seventeen

FRANK JUMPED back as a wall of boxes cascaded to the floor in front of him and Joe. He could just make out Paul Dupre racing down the gravel drive toward Bourbon Street.

"Quick! We've got to get him!" Joe cried.

Frank lost his footing and fell as he tried to avoid the boxes. By the time Frank pulled himself to his feet, Joe was already leaping over the boxes to race after Paul. Jumping into action, Frank scrambled over the cartons after them. "I'm right behind you, Joe!"

Frank rounded the corner of the drive in time to see Joe launch into a flying tackle that caught Paul Dupre by the waist. The two of them crashed to the gravel in a tangle of arms and legs. Frank caught up to them as they rolled to a stop. Grabbing Dupre's arms, he twisted them behind his back. The man struggled, trying to twist free, but he was no match for the Hardys.

"Give it up," Joe said, heaving for breath.

It wasn't until they led Paul Dupre back to the carriage house that Frank remembered Danielle. She was standing in front of the open carriage house door. "Uncle Paul, how could you do it?" she asked angrily.

Paul Dupre looked down, not meeting his niece's gaze. At least the guy had the decency to act sheepish, thought Frank.

"Hugh Gatlin owes me," Paul finally said. "I've been dreaming of getting even ever since he sold his share of the club to that thief Marsden. It wasn't until I ran into a friend of mine who played poker with Mike Keyes that I thought of how to do it. I figured if Mike was as deeply in debt as my friend said—"

"Then he'd be open to the idea of stealing from his boss, Hugh Gatlin," Joe finished. "Gee, you're a real humanitarian, helping Mike out of his money troubles that way," he added sarcastically.

Dupre simply glared as Frank and Joe led him to the carriage house and made him sit against the wall. Frank found some twine, and he used it to tie Dupre's wrists and ankles.

"But, Uncle Paul, you weren't on the boat during the evening cruise," Danielle said, crouching next to him. "How did you get on board to steal the money?"

"It was easy," her uncle said with a shrug. "Mike had told me he'd leave the motorboat moored to a deserted warehouse dock upriver. All I had to do was find the boat and steer downriver to the *Delta Princess* pier. The riverboat was just getting in when I arrived. The *Princess* is so big, I didn't think anyone would notice a small motorboat tied up right behind her. There was a huge crowd coming off the riverboat, everyone all hyped up after the night in the casino. I walked right on to the boat without attracting attention."

"Mike must have told you where the safe was," Joe put in.

Paul Dupre nodded. "He'd left some plastic explosives on the motorboat for me to use, too. The upper level was deserted, just like Mike said it would be. Mike stood outside the room where the safe was, just in case anyone heard the explosion. Afterward, he gave himself a tap on the back of the head with a metal pipe he'd brought along, just to make the whole thing look good. Of course, by then I had already taken off down the outside deck—"

"Right past J. J. Johnson," Frank put in.

"Yes," Dupre said. "At first I panicked when I saw a man standing there. But once I realized it was J. J. and that he couldn't see me, I hustled past him and climbed down the paddle wheel to the motorboat. Then I was gone."

So far Paul Dupre's story fit what he and Joe had guessed, thought Frank. "So, when Mike came by here the next day, it was to pick up his half of the money, *not* to carry out some scheme for Hugh Gatlin," he said.

"Except I fouled up the rendezvous when I spotted Mike behind the club," Joe added.

Dupre glowered at Joe and shifted uncomfortably against the carriage house wall. "I knew you two were trouble the second I saw you. I'm just sorry Mike didn't hit you with that railing when he had the chance!"

"Uncle Paul!" Danielle exclaimed, her mouth falling open.

"Sorry, Danielle, but your uncle is obviously a bigger sleazebag than you thought—not to mention greedy enough to commit murder," Joe said.

Crossing his arms over his chest, Joe turned back to Dupre. "What happened? You decided you deserved *all* the money? Is that why you killed Mike?"

Dupre snapped to attention, and the defiant look drained from his face. "You can't pin *that* on me. I'm not the one who killed Mike."

"Yeah, right," Frank scoffed. "Next you'll try to convince us you never stole the money, either, *or* tried to kill Nancy and me with that water moccasin out at Mama Gayle's Boat Rental." He kicked at the tires of the green station wagon, which still had traces of mud on them.

"Okay, so maybe I *did* put the water moccasin in the boat," Dupre muttered.

"It's my fault," Danielle said, looking up at Frank and Joe with troubled eyes. "J. J. told me y'all were going to check out a place called Mama Gayle's out at Big Bayou Black. I guess I shouldn't have mentioned it to Uncle Paul, but I never thought it would cause any trouble."

Frank could see how hard it was for Danielle to

accept that her uncle was capable of such awful things. Turning back to Dupre, he said, "We didn't see your car at Mama Gayle's."

"I wasn't about to make an announcement that I was there," Dupre said dryly. "I drove past the lot, then parked by the side of the road and came through the woods. The trees come right up close to the lake, and the shed windows were open. It didn't take a genius to figure out which boat you'd be looking for. I planted the snake under the tarp, then climbed back out one of the windows." He let out a chuckle and shook his head. "Just in time, too. You and your friend got to the shed right after that."

"So it *was* you I heard," Frank said, thinking back.

"Yes." Dupre's nervous gaze shot back and forth between Frank and Joe. "But I didn't kill Mike, I swear it." He must have seen the doubt in Frank and Joe's eyes because he quickly added, "The last time I saw Mike was Saturday night. He came by the club after the *Princess* docked for the night. We split up the money, and that was that. When he left, he was alive." Paul nodded toward the fan, which still lay overturned on a table at the back of the carriage house. "Count the money if you don't believe me. You'll only find half of what was stolen."

That would be easy enough to check, thought Frank. And Dupre didn't seem to have a black Jeep like the one he and Joe had seen just before finding Mike's body. "The police are the ones you'll have to convince, not us," he told Paul.

"I guess I'd better call them," Danielle said. She leveled a long, sad look at her uncle, then went into the club through the back door.

"There's still a huge, unanswered question," Frank said, turning to Joe. "If Dupre *didn't* kill Mike, then who did?"

Joe frowned. Grabbing Frank's elbow, he pulled him out of Dupre's hearing range. "Do you think his murder could be related to the takeover of BayouTech by Deutsche Industries?"

"Could be," Frank said. "Nancy and Bess are at Gatlin's office now, watching the security tape. If Mike had anything to do with the message about the takeover winding up in Remy's bag, they'll probably see it."

"In the meantime"—Joe shot a pointed look in Paul Dupre's direction—"it can't hurt to find out if *he* saw anything."

Turning back to Dupre, Frank raised his voice and asked, "Did anything else happen when you were on the riverboat Friday night? Anything at all out of the ordinary?"

The man stared at him. "Why should I help *you?*" he asked.

"If you cooperate with the investigation, you might get less of a jail sentence," Frank said.

Dupre was silent for a minute. Then he gave a sigh and said, "It's not like I was on the riverboat long enough to get into the social scene. I went straight to the office where the safe was. The only thing I heard the entire time was some bozo who decided to make friends with Mike right before I blew open the safe. Mike got rid of him pretty fast, though."

"You didn't mention that before," Joe said, jolting to attention. "What did the guy say?"

"I didn't hear every word, what with the office door closed and all," Paul said, shrugging. "But it was quiet enough to make out most of what they said. The man was looking for an envelope and wanted to know if Mike had it."

Frank caught the meaningful look Joe gave him. Maybe Mike *had* been involved in passing word of the BayouTech takeover! "What did Mike tell the guy?" Frank asked.

"Mike said there'd been a delay. Then he sent the guy back to the casino," Paul said. "I figured he just said anything to get rid of him so that he wouldn't foul up our heist."

"Mmm" was all Frank said. He wasn't about to tell Paul his suspicions of what Mike was *really* up to. "Did you see the man? Did Mike say his name?"

Paul shrugged. "I wasn't about to stick my head out the door while I had the safe open," he said. "But Mike did say something. Let's see . . . what was it he called him?" Paul frowned, then said, "Mr. J., that was it."

Mr. J., eh? Frank thought. It wasn't much to go on, but there *was* one person he could think of with that initial. "Bill Jacobson?" he asked Joe.

"Could be," Joe said. "We should tell Nancy."

"She's probably still at Gatlin's office," said

Frank. "Let's call—as soon as the police take Paul into custody."

After leaving the Royal Creole, Nancy, Bess, and Shelley decided to make one more attempt to speak with Lisa Thibaud. When they reached Thibaud's Creole Kitchen, Ms. Thibaud was there. Her large frame filled the doorway as the three girls approached the restaurant.

"Let's get one thing straight," she called, her voice booming down the sidewalk. "There's nothing I want from you, and nothing I'm about to give you. So why don't y'all just keep right on walking right past my restaurant."

"We can't, Ms. Thibaud," Shelley said. Her voice was trembling as she, Nancy, and Bess stopped at the front door of the restaurant. Nancy had to admire her friend as Shelley went on. "If you'd just tell us why you were outside my husband's restaurant on Friday afternoon, we will leave you alone for good. But we've got to know why you were there."

"I already told you, honey. I was just stopping by to wish Remy good luck on his opening night. When you girls saw me, I was looking in the back window because there were no lights on in the kitchen. There's no harm in looking, is there?"

"No," Bess said boldly. "But there is harm in ruining the special cake Remy made for the opening."

"I had nothing to do with that!" Ms. Thibaud said hotly. Then she let out a long sigh. "You might as well come in," she said, stepping aside so Nancy,

Bess, and Shelley could enter the restaurant. "I'll tell you my part of the story, since I can tell you won't leave me alone till I do."

Ms. Thibaud eased herself into a chair. "It's no secret that my restaurant hasn't been doing well recently. And with Remy opening his place down the block, I knew I was in for it. Still, when you saw me on Friday, I *had* come to wish Remy well. But when I saw that no one was there—*and* that the back door was open—well, I just let myself in. I did see that smashed cake you were talking about. But I didn't smash it. What I did do, though, was memorize a couple of recipes I saw on a counter by the kitchen window."

"How dare you steal my husband's recipes!" Shelley shouted.

"I know, dear, and I'm sorry. New Orleans is a tough town," she continued. "I'm not the first person to steal someone's recipes, and I won't be the last. The truth is, I didn't want Remy to fail; I just wanted my place to do better. And when I saw those recipes sitting there, well, I just couldn't help myself. Once I memorized a few recipes, I pushed the button lock, then closed the door behind me. When I heard you girls coming, I panicked and ran into the bushes."

Nancy, Bess, and Shelley were silent while they took in the information. "That explains one thing," Nancy said after a minute. "The kitchen showed no sign of forced entry when we discovered the cake had been smashed. And whoever smashed it," she added "either must have had a key—"

"Or else Remy left the door open in his rush to

get to Bill Jacobson's office," Shelley finished for her.

The three girls thanked Lisa Thibaud for her time and her honesty. "We promise not to bother you again," Shelley said at the door.

"Don't be silly," Ms. Thibaud said with a hearty laugh. "Ya'll come to dinner at my place real soon. And bring that husband of yours," she added with a chuckle. "I'm going to cook you some of my *own* Creole specialties. I promise."

"Well, that clears up Lisa Thibaud's connection to the Creole Kitchen," Bess said a few minutes later as they walked down the sidewalk. "I must say I feel sorry for her."

"It certainly rules her out as a suspect in our case. But it doesn't leave us anywhere. We still don't know who ruined the cake and wrecked the kitchen."

"It leaves us nowhere," Shelley said with a sigh. "Maybe something on the casino's videotape will help us."

Half an hour later, Nancy, Bess, and Shelley were sitting in Hugh Gatlin's riverside office.

"Okay, the security tape is set up," Faye said. She turned from the TV screen and looked at Nancy, Bess, and Shelley. "Are you ready?"

Since the Hardys were busy that morning, Faye had offered to come with the girls. Hugh Gatlin was at a conference of local businessmen, delivering the speech he had been preparing over the weekend, so they had all settled into the antique chairs and sofa of his corner office.

"We're ready," Nancy said.

Bess nodded toward the VCR. "Let's roll it!"

Faye hit a button on the remote, then sat cross-legged on the plush carpeting to watch. As the grainy black-and-white scene of a gambling room came into focus, Nancy focused all her attention on what was happening on the screen.

"There's Remy," Shelley said. "He sure doesn't look happy."

That was the understatement of the year, Nancy thought. Remy was sitting in front of the blackjack table with a desperate expression on his handsome face. His dark hair was matted to his sweaty forehead, and he kept looking at his cards every two seconds.

"I don't see his canvas bag," Bess said.

"He said it was on the floor next to him. That's out of the camera's range," Nancy pointed out.

Shelley gasped as they all watched Remy suddenly grab the blackjack dealer's shirt. "Poor Remy. He's been under so much pressure."

"Here comes Mike," Nancy said. He looked formidable on the videotape as he pulled Remy away from the blackjack dealer. As she watched, she thought that it hardly seemed possible that now Mike was dead.

Shaking herself, Nancy tried to concentrate on every detail. "Hey!" she said suddenly. "Isn't that something sticking out of Mike's shirt pocket?"

The scene at the blackjack table was so fast and chaotic, she wasn't a hundred percent sure she'd taken it all in. "Could we rewind and go over that part again?" she asked, turning to Faye.

"No problem. In fact, let's try it in slow motion." Faye hit the buttons on the remote, and seconds later the same scene unfolded again. This time, as Mike pulled Remy from the dealer, Mike's jacket shifted so that Nancy was able to get a clear view of his shirt pocket underneath.

"It *is* an envelope!" Bess breathed. "And look!"

In the scuffle, Remy's hands flailed wildly at Mike. He latched onto Mike's shirt for just a minute, but it was enough to knock the envelope from Mike's pocket. Nancy held her breath, following the envelope with her eyes as it fell in slow motion, disappearing out of sight behind the blackjack table. "I bet anything it fell right into Remy's bag," she murmured. "If only we could know for sure!"

Moments later the video showed Remy bending down toward the floor. He picked up a canvas bag—exactly where the envelope had fallen. As he slung the straps over his shoulder, Nancy was able to see the chef's hat printed on the bag. Then Remy stormed from the casino.

"Check it out," Faye said. "Doesn't that guy look familiar?" She jumped over to the console and pointed to a man standing among the crowd of people behind the blackjack table. He had a barrel-chested build and a shaggy beard Nancy recognized right away.

"Bill Jacobson!" Shelley breathed. "What would *he* be doing on the *Delta Princess?*"

From what Nancy could see, Jacobson wasn't even gambling. He kept glancing around and checking his watch. "It looks like he's waiting for someone," she said. "Or some*thing.*"

"Like maybe an envelope with advance word of the BayouTech takeover?" Faye suggested.

"Exactly," Nancy said.

She turned as the phone on Hugh Gatlin's desk rang. Reaching over, Faye picked up the receiver and said, "Hello?" Her entire face lit up, and a moment later, Nancy knew why. "Hi, Frank!" Faye said brightly. "What's up? . . . He confessed? That's great!"

Nancy exchanged glances with Bess and Shelley. "Sounds as if they've had a break in their case," Nancy said, while Faye continued talking on the phone. "But I wonder *who* confessed?"

"Paul Dupre," Faye told her, cupping her hand over the receiver and holding it out to Nancy. "He and Mike stole the money from the *Delta Princess.* Frank and Joe are still trying to figure out who killed Mike, but Frank says he has some information for you that could be important."

Nancy took the receiver, and said, "Congratulations, Frank. It's nice to know that at least *one* of our cases is solved."

"Yup. Listen, Dupre heard something while he was cracking open Gatlin's safe," Frank said. "Some guy tracked down Mike and asked for an envelope."

"Makes sense. Mike *was* carrying the envelope that turned up in Remy's bag," Nancy told him. "We just saw it on the security tape. Sounds like maybe Mike was supposed to turn over the envelope to someone else, if someone was asking for it. Does Paul Dupre know who the person was?"

"Dupre didn't see him, but he heard Mike call the man Mr. J.," Frank's voice came back over the line.

"Bill Jacobson," Nancy said excitedly. "We just spotted him on the security tape. Looks as if he could be the person meant to receive the note about the takeover of BayouTech." Her mind raced as she tried to fit together all the pieces of the puzzle. "But we still don't know how Mike got the information. Maybe we'll find out more when we stake out Jacobson's rendezvous at the cemetery tonight."

"I can't believe we're going into a cemetery in the middle of the night," Bess whispered that evening, as she, Nancy, and Shelley approached the gates of Old St. Louis Cemetery Number 1. "Are we crazy?"

Nancy flicked on her penlight as they went through the cemetery gates. "Maybe," she said. "This place *is* pretty creepy."

Old-fashioned lanterns cast an eerie light over the brick and marble vaults inside. Statues of angels and cherubs loomed over many of the vaults, like ghosts in the night. Everywhere Nancy looked, there were crumbling gravestones, toppled masonry, and thick black shadows that shifted with the breeze. Nancy couldn't help feeling as if they'd walked into a vampire movie.

"It's not the kind of place where I'd choose to spend time," she whispered. "That must be what Jacobson was counting on when he picked such a creepy place to meet. At least all these raised vaults give us plenty of hiding places."

"The ground in New Orleans is too swampy to allow for burial underground, so all the cemeteries have above-ground vaults," Shelley explained in a whisper. "St. Louis Number One is one of the oldest cemeteries in the city. It dates back to the seventeen hundreds." She shot a nervous look over her shoulder before adding, "Maybe I shouldn't tell you this, but there's even a famous voodoo queen buried here, Marie Laveau."

"A voodoo queen?" Bess echoed, glancing left and right. "That's not the most comforting thing to know, especially after the way Angela Dixon threatened you the other night, Shelley."

"Bill Jacobson is the one we need to look out for, not someone who's been dead for over two hundred years," Nancy said. "Anyway, Frank, Joe, and Faye are waiting just outside. If anything *does* happen, all we have to do is yell." The Hardys and Faye were keeping an eye on the entrance from Faye's car, which was parked just down Basin Street, in front of one of the housing projects surrounding the cemetery.

Nancy shone the beam of her penlight on a raised vault not far from the entrance. "We can keep an eye on the gates from there," she said, heading for it. Once she, Bess, and Shelley had crouched behind the vault, she clicked off her penlight. Every noise echoed eerily around them: the breeze ruffling through the wisteria against the back wall, a bird calling from one of the live oaks, even the sound of their own breathing.

"Remind me *never* to do this again," Bess said.

"Shhhh!" Nancy hissed, cocking her head to the side. She thought she'd heard something behind them, but when she looked over her shoulder, all she saw was the black shadow of a vault.

She turned back to the entrance just as a shadowy figure came through the gates. He passed beneath a lamp, and Nancy clearly recognized Bill Jacobson. Several yards inside the entrance, he stopped in front of a raised vault with pillars.

So far, so good, thought Nancy. He doesn't seem to know we're here. Now, all we have to do is wait and see who he's meeting.

Suddenly she heard a scuffling noise *behind* her. She whirled around, then gasped as a hulking black figure jumped from behind a gravestone a few feet away.

"What—" she cried out.

Nancy couldn't see anything except a dark blur rushing toward her. Long arms lifted something into the air. In a flash, she glimpsed the blue-gray gleam of a metal shovel blade.

"No!" she cried.

But the figure was already bringing the shovel crashing toward her head.

Chapter

Eighteen

"THAT WAS NANCY!" Joe cried, as a scream echoed from inside Old St. Louis Cemetery Number 1.

He threw open the back door of Faye's car and leaped out onto the sidewalk, his eyes fixed on the cemetery gates. A second later Frank and Faye flew out of the front seats.

"Bill Jacobson just went in there," Faye said anxiously. "Sounds like he's causing trouble."

"Well, if he's looking for trouble," Frank said, balling his hands into fists, "he found it. Come on!" Joe was already pounding toward the gates. He'd only gone a few yards when he saw Jacobson streak from the cemetery and run the other way down Basin Street. "I'm after him!" Joe yelled.

"We'll check on Nancy," Frank's voice came from behind Joe.

Joe took off after Jacobson. Even though the critic was about twenty yards ahead, he was out of shape and not able to run that fast. Joe was gaining on him. He saw Jacobson throw a panicked look over his shoulder. As soon as he spotted Joe, Jacobson angled across Basin Street, heading for a path that wound into the housing projects. Even from fifteen yards back, Joe could see that Jacobson was sweaty and winded.

"That's what you get for eating all that rich cooking," Joe muttered, pouring on more speed. "Face it. A cream puff like you is no match for Joe Hardy." Ahead, a handful of teenagers were sitting on the stoop of one of the buildings, listening to a huge boom box from which rap music blasted at top volume. As Jacobson reached them, he stopped short and yanked the box away from them.

"Hey! What are you doing!" one of the teens demanded.

Jacobson whirled around and, letting out a guttural cry, hurled the box at Joe. Joe was moving so fast he didn't realize what was happening until the boom box was whizzing toward him. He tried to jump out of the way, but the box caught him right below the knee.

"Ouch!" The impact threw him off balance, and Joe tumbled onto the cement walk, clutching his shin.

"Are you all right?" one of the teenagers asked.

Ignoring the shooting pain in his leg, Joe scrambled to his feet. "Couldn't be better," he grunted out.

Joe saw Jacobson disappearing between two

buildings of the housing project. When Joe followed, he found himself in a run-down courtyard at the center of the buildings. Dozens of people were talking and laughing in small clusters, and a group of kids were playing dodgeball. Bill Jacobson was nowhere in sight.

"Anyone see a man run through here just now?" Joe called. "He has a beard."

Half a dozen people pointed in different directions. Joe let out a sigh. With so much activity going on in the courtyard already, it wasn't surprising that no one had paid close attention to Bill Jacobson. Looking around, Joe saw there were three different paths leading out of the courtyard. Jacobson could have taken any one of them. By now, he was long gone.

With a sigh, Joe shoved his hands in his pockets and walked back to Basin Street. He was crossing to the other side when the screech of tires made him look up the street. Joe did a double take when he saw the vehicle that was just pulling out of a parking spot at top speed. It was a black Jeep!

As the Jeep careened past him, Joe spun around, trying to get a look at the driver. But all he saw was the driver's blurred silhouette. Within moments, the Jeep streaked out of sight down Basin Street.

Joe stared after the Jeep, frowning. He himself had taken the only path from the courtyard to Basin Street. The other three paths all led in other directions; Jacobson wouldn't have had time to double back here so quickly.

"But if that guy *wasn't* Jacobson," he wondered aloud, "who was he?"

When Joe reached the cemetery, he found Nancy sitting on the ground next to a raised vault not far from the entrance, rubbing her ankle. Frank, Faye, Shelley, and Bess were crouched around her. "What happened?" Joe asked. "Nancy, are you all right?"

"Twisted ankle," she said, trying to smile.

"It happened when we had to dive out of the way of a shovel-wielding maniac," Bess added. As she turned to look up at Joe, he saw the grim expression in her eyes. "She's lucky she was able to dive out of the way."

Nancy rotated her ankle. "I'll be fine," she said. "I just wish the fall hadn't kept me from finding out who the person was."

"It wasn't Bill Jacobson? He ran out of here right after you screamed," Joe said, as he and Frank helped Nancy to her feet. Frowning, he added, "Sorry, you guys, but he got away."

"It wasn't Jacobson," Shelley said. "We were watching him when someone *else* attacked us from behind."

Moving gingerly, Nancy walked over to some tombstones behind the raised vault where she'd been sitting. She flicked on her penlight, shining it carefully over the low brick vaults near the wall.

"There's the shovel," Faye said, pointing.

As Joe followed, he caught sight of a metal shovel next to the vaults. Thick vines of lavender wisteria twisted up the cemetery wall behind. As Nancy's flashlight beam played over the vines, Joe saw that some of the flowers were crushed.

"That must be how the person got away. He

climbed right over the wall," he said. "I think I spotted the guy—or his car, anyway. When I was coming back here after chasing Jacobson, a black Jeep tore down Canal Street."

"You're kidding!" Frank jolted to attention. Joe could practically see the wheels turning inside his head. "So, whoever Jacobson was meeting is the same person we saw right before we found Mike's body."

"What we still *don't* know is who the person is," Shelley said.

"And we still can't be sure Bill Jacobson is the 'Mr. J.' who asked Mike for an envelope on the *Delta Princess*," Faye added. *"Or* that he's the one who was supposed to get the information about the takeover of BayouTech by Deutsche Industries."

Bess frowned thoughtfully and looked around the group. "What about Angela Dixon? Do you think she could have leaked the takeover information to get back at Remy?" she asked. "Maybe she planned to give Jacobson advance word of the takeover in exchange for his giving the Royal Creole a bad review."

"Which could seriously hurt the restaurant's chances for success," Shelley finished, frowning. "It's possible."

"You guys, I found something!" Nancy called out.

When Joe turned around, he saw that Nancy was reaching into the thick wisteria vines. She straightened up and held out a slip of pink paper.

"Looks like a dry-cleaning receipt," Bess said.

Nancy nodded. "Whoever attacked us must have

dropped it in his hurry to get away." Squinting at the letters printed on top, she read, "'R and S Cleaners.' They're located on Tchoupitoulas Street."

"Isn't that the street where the BayouTech office is?" Joe asked.

Shelley nodded as she leaned over Nancy's shoulder to look at the receipt. "The customer's name isn't written down, but it says here the person had a suit cleaned."

"That doesn't exactly narrow the field of suspects," Frank said. "Angela Dixon, Randall Legarde, and every other person who works at BayouTech probably wears suits."

"True, but someone at the dry cleaners may be able to tell us more about who the order is for," Nancy said. She folded up the receipt and put it in her jeans pocket. "It can't hurt to pay a visit to the cleaners and find out."

"Anything Frank and I can do to help?" Joe asked.

"We won't know until after we visit the dry cleaners tomorrow morning. Maybe we should meet up afterward, say around ten o'clock?"

"Good idea. I'm sure Remy will want to know what's going on, too, so let's all meet at the Creole Garden," Shelley suggested. Brushing back her straight blond hair, she shot a hopeful smile around the group. "With any luck, we'll get to the bottom of Mike's murder *and* the attacks on Remy."

Nancy took a deep breath as she, Bess, and Shelley paused outside R&S Cleaners the following morning. "Here goes nothing," she murmured, raising an eyebrow at Shelley and Bess. Then she pulled open the door and went inside.

A woman with dark hair, tawny skin, and almond-shaped eyes smiled at them from behind the counter. Hundreds of cellophane-wrapped clothes hung on a rotating rack behind her. "Good morning. Can I help you?" the woman asked.

Nancy handed over the receipt, and the woman flipped a switch, setting the rack of clothes into motion. After a few moments, she stopped the rack, plucked a plastic-wrapped item from it, and brought it to the counter.

"A blue and white seersucker suit—a man's," Shelley murmured, frowning. "Haven't we seen someone wearing something seersucker lately?"

The suit *did* look familiar, thought Nancy. But she couldn't place it.

"I think you'll be pleased with the job we did," the woman behind the counter said, breaking into Nancy's thoughts. She lifted the plastic and pointed proudly to the right sleeve of the seersucker jacket. "We were able to completely remove the icing stains."

"Icing stains?" Shelley repeated. She turned to Nancy and Bess, her brown eyes flashing with excitement. "Doesn't that make you think of—"

"Remy's cake!" Nancy breathed.

"You guys, I just remembered something!" Bess said, grabbing Nancy's arm. "Right after the cake was destroyed, Mr. Legarde showed up, wearing a navy jacket and blue-and-white *seersucker* slacks!"

Nancy glanced at the woman behind the counter,

who was looking at them in confusion. "Why don't we talk outside?" Nancy suggested.

Smiling at the woman, she said, "Sorry, but we, uh, can't take the suit right now. Someone will be back for it later." Then she, Bess, and Shelley hurried outside.

"I don't get it," Shelley said, as they started to walk toward the Royal Creole. "Are you trying to say that Mr. Legarde smashed Remy's cake?"

"He must have," Nancy said. "I remember him wearing the seersucker slacks, too. I bet he was wearing the matching jacket and then had to change after he smashed Remy's cake."

"Think about it," Bess said. "Mr. Legarde is a pretty formal dresser. Every other time we've seen him, he's worn suits. He just doesn't seem like a mix-and-match kind of a guy."

Shelley still looked confused. "But Mr. Legarde is Remy's financial backer. Why would he do anything that could hurt the restaurant's chances of success?"

"I'm not sure," Nancy admitted. She closed her eyes, trying to make sense of it all. "If Mr. Legarde is the one who dropped this receipt, then he must be the person who attacked me with the shovel. I bet anything he's the person Bill Jacobson was meeting at the cemetery."

"Which means that he's also the Mr. Redgale who uses the answering service," Bess added.

"Think about it." Nancy closed her eyes, picturing the name in her mind. "When you rearrange the letters in Redgale, you get Legarde! If Mr. Legarde is using the answering service under a bogus name, he must be up to something funny. And chances are, Mike Keyes and Bill Jacobson were in on it, since they both used the answering service to contact Mr. Legarde."

Shelley frowned, looking back and forth between Nancy and Bess. "Do you think Mr. Legarde was driving the Jeep?" she asked. "I mean, I hate to think it, but what if he's the person who killed Mike?"

"Could be," Nancy said. "We know Mike had the envelope containing the message about the takeover of BayouTech by Deutsche Industries. If Mr. Legarde *provided* the information, he might have decided to kill Mike for some reason after the envelope got lost." She took a deep breath and let it out slowly. "What I still don't get is *why* Legarde would bother to leak the information in the first place."

The girls had been walking while they talked, and now they turned onto Royal Street. Nancy could spot the awning of the Royal Creole a block ahead. "Maybe when we talk to Remy, Frank, and Joe, we'll be able to come up with an explanation that makes sense," she said.

Nancy was vaguely aware of a car pulling up to the curb next to her. It wasn't until she heard Bess gasp that she looked at the vehicle.

It was a shiny black Jeep.

"Oh, no," she breathed.

The driver's door flew open, and Randall Legarde got out. One quick stride and he was right in front of them. Before Nancy could move, he reached out and grabbed her by the arm.

"Mr. Legarde!" she said, trying to stifle the fear that welled up inside of her. "What a surprise!"

"Don't pull that innocent act with me," Legarde said, fixing her with an evil glare. "I found out from the dry cleaners that three girls turned in the ticket for my suit. It didn't take a genius to figure out it was you," he spat out. "You've caused enough trouble nosing into affairs that don't concern you, and I'm putting a stop to it—now."

Nancy caught the looks of dread Bess and Shelley both shot her. She was about to twist away from Mr. Legarde when she caught sight of the revolver he held in his other hand, barely concealed in his jacket pocket.

"Do exactly as I say," he said in a voice that told Nancy he was all business, "or you're dead."

Chapter

Nineteen

FRANK, JOE, AND FAYE were about a block from the Royal Creole when Frank saw the Jeep pull over to the curb ahead, next to Nancy, Bess, and Shelley.

"Joe! Check it out." Frank stopped short on the sidewalk, his eyes fixed on the tall man who got out of the Jeep. "That's Randall Legarde!"

"So *he's* the one I saw driving away from the cemetery," Joe said. *"And* the one who almost ran us down before we found Mike's body."

Frank nodded. His mind was spinning with theories about Mike's death and the leak of information about the takeover of BayouTech, but there wasn't time to hash it out now. "I don't like the way he's holding on to Nancy. Something's up."

Faye turned to Frank, a worried expression on her face. "Shouldn't we do something?"

Up ahead, Frank could see Mr. Legarde escorting the three girls into the Jeep. "I'm not sure what's going on, but it's definitely trouble," he said. "If he's got a gun—and he must have, or Nancy wouldn't go with him—we can't just run down the street after him. He's liable to kill one of the girls."

"So what are we going to do?" Faye whispered. Frank and Joe looked at each other and said in unison, "We'll grab a cab and follow them!"

Nancy sat motionless in the backseat of the Jeep, squeezed in next to Shelley and Bess. After ushering them into the Jeep, Randall Legarde had quickly tied each girl's hands together with rope he had in the Jeep. Then he'd climbed behind the wheel and started driving. Every time Nancy saw the cold, angry expression on his face in the rearview mirror, the knot in her stomach twisted a notch tighter. She couldn't see Legarde's pistol, but she knew it had to be within his easy reach.

Looking out the window, Nancy saw that Mr. Legarde was driving out of the French Quarter north on Tulane Avenue. "Where are we going?" she asked.

"You'll find out soon enough," the man answered. He shifted his eyes from the road long enough to glare at Nancy in the rearview mirror. "Some place where you won't be able to foul up my plan anymore."

"Which plan is that? The one to leak advance word of the takeover of BayouTech by Deutsche Industries?" Nancy asked. Legarde's scowl told her she'd guessed correctly, so she went on. "Someone could really cash in on that information. If they bought BayouTech stock now, before the official announcement of the buyout, they'd make a killing when the stock rises after the news is made public."

"Bravo, Nancy," Mr. Legarde said dryly. "You have a good grasp of economic principles."

"You mean, of insider trading!" Bess blurted out. "You could go to jail, Mr. Legarde."

"*If* I get caught," he answered. "And I'm not about to let that happen."

Again, his cold gaze swept over Nancy, Shelley, and Bess, and Nancy couldn't stifle the shiver that swept through her. Glancing out the window, she saw that they were heading out of the main part of the city on the Pontchartrain Expressway. She didn't know what he had in store for them, but she doubted it was a picnic in the countryside.

"I can't believe it," Shelley said, breaking into Nancy's thoughts. "You *are* the one who wrote the note we found in Remy's bag."

"You must have gotten Mike Keyes to deliver the information," Nancy added. Seeing the look of surprise on Legarde's face, she explained, "The security tape from the *Delta Princess* shows the envelope in Mike's pocket. We saw it get knocked into Remy's bag. By the time Mike realized the envelope was gone, it must have been too late to get it back."

Legarde shook his head in disgust. "I never should have trusted Mike," he said, frowning.

"We saw Bill Jacobson on the security tape, too,"

Nancy went on. "He's the person Mike was supposed to give the information *to,* isn't he?" Mr. Legarde didn't deny it. "What I don't understand is, why? I mean, you'll already profit from the takeover, since your company will be worth so much more. Why risk going to jail by passing along information that could be used in insider trading?"

Mr. Legarde leveled a long look at Nancy in the mirror but said nothing.

"I can't believe Remy ever got mixed up with you," Shelley muttered, shaking her head in disgust. "You're nothing but a crook!"

"I'm a businessman!" Legarde shot back. "Everything I did was for Remy, for the success of the Royal Creole."

Nancy blinked as his words sank in. All of a sudden, she was almost sure she understood Randall Legarde's motivation! "The Royal Creole *is* important to you," she murmured. "And Bill Jacobson can give you one thing you *won't* be getting from the buyout by Deutsche Industries. . . ."

"A good review!" Bess put in. "Of course!"

As soon as Nancy saw the look on Mr. Legarde's face, she knew she was right. "An eminent food critic like Bill Jacobson doesn't take bribes every day," he said, after a long pause. "I knew I'd have to approach him carefully. When I first called him, I got him to see that as a major player in the business world, I could offer him bigger opportunities than he'd ever dreamed of. I was vague, of course—I wasn't about to incriminate myself. But Jacobson was smart enough to understand what I was getting at. He agreed to at least see what I had to offer."

"Why didn't you just ask him over the phone, instead of having Mike passing the information to him?" Bess asked.

"I didn't get to be one of the top players in Louisiana by taking stupid risks," Legarde said coolly. "Phones could be tapped, or if we'd met, someone could see us. So I insisted on using a courier. That way no one could connect the two of us. All contact had to be made through a third party."

"The A-One Answering Service," Nancy said. "But how did you choose Mike Keyes as courier?"

"The Keyeses are an old New Orleans family," Mr. Legarde answered. "I've attended social functions with them ever since I can remember. Mike was the black sheep of the family, always getting into trouble. Last year, his parents cut him off financially, told him to get his act together."

"But he didn't?" Shelley guessed.

"No," Mr. Legarde said, shaking his head. "When he came to me and asked to borrow some money, I couldn't say no. Asking him to act as courier seemed an easy enough way for him to repay the debt."

"Except that he screwed up," Nancy said. "You must have been furious when he lost the envelope."

Legarde frowned before answering. "I hoped to get it back before Remy discovered it. I called and set up that bogus interview with Bill Jacobson, then sneaked into the restaurant. As Remy's financial backer, I have a key to the front door. But I was in a hurry, and I got careless. I slammed into the cake with my arm while I was looking around the kitchen. After that, I had to get out of there. I couldn't afford to be seen with cake all over me. Luckily, I had a clean jacket in my car. Remy never suspected I was responsible for the mishap."

As Nancy listened, more and more pieces of the puzzle fell into place. "Then did you come back to the Royal Creole later that night to try again?"

"No," Mr. Legarde answered. "That was Mike. He knocked out Remy and took the bag from the National Culinary Institute convention."

"Then he tore the kitchen apart so Remy would think it was sabotage?" Nancy guessed.

"Yes. Mike didn't realize the envelope wasn't there until after he left," Mr. Legarde said, shaking his head. "It was just a lucky break that Jacobson stopped by the restaurant that same night and glimpsed you three with Remy, as well as some of the damage that had been done. When he contacted me through the service and described you, I knew it would just be a matter of time before you found the envelope. I let him know I was afraid you might be trouble. When you approached him at Commander's Palace the next day, he knew you were up to something."

"So Bill Jacobson must have been the one who pushed you from the St. Charles Avenue streetcar, Nancy," Shelley said. "And the one who put the oleander blossoms in your salad at the Chartres Street Bistro, too."

Mr. Legarde gave a curt nod, then slammed his palm against the steering wheel in a sudden outburst. "You would have ruined everything for us—and it was all because of Mike's stupidity!"

"Is that why you killed him?" Nancy asked, shooting Mr. Legarde a probing look.

He glowered at her in the mirror. "Mike tried to be clever," he said. "His instructions were to deliver the information to Jacobson. Not only did he fail to do that, but he took it upon himself to steam open the envelope and read the contents. He arranged a meeting—"

"At the Riverside construction site?" Bess asked.

"Yes," Mr. Legarde answered. "Mike had already cut the lock on the gate when I got there, so I drove right in. I couldn't believe he had the nerve to threaten me. He said he'd expose me to the police unless I paid him fifty thousand dollars! That was when I decided he was too much of a liability."

"So you killed him." Nancy couldn't believe how outraged Mr. Legarde sounded. He made it seem as if Mike was the only one breaking the law, but as far as she was concerned, Legarde's crimes were far worse.

Taking another look out the window, Nancy saw that they had left the highway and were driving around a huge lake. "Where are we?" she asked.

"Lake Pontchartrain," Shelley said, her eyes filled with fear.

As they drove, houses became more and more sparse and the shoreline more ragged and swamp-like. Nancy, Bess, and Shelley exchanged grim looks when Mr. Legarde finally turned onto a rutted dirt road. He drove about a hundred yards, stopped, and turned off the motor.

Uh-oh, thought Nancy. The area was teeming with wildlife, but she didn't see a single person.

"What are we doing here?" Bess asked.

"You'll find out soon enough," Legarde answered. As he got out of the Jeep and opened the back door, sunlight glimmered on the pistol in his hand. "Everyone out," he ordered.

Nancy's wrists were numb from being tied together. As she, Bess, and Shelley stumbled out of the car, she said, "You won't get away with this. Frank, Joe, and Remy are waiting for us at the Royal Creole. They'll call the police if we don't show up."

"By the time they do," Mr. Legarde said, "you three—and the evidence linking me to any insider trading and to Mike's death—will be long gone."

Nancy shivered at the cold, calculated way he spoke. Gesturing with his pistol, Legarde led them off the path into the overgrown woods. The ground was muddy, and the three girls stumbled several times when their shoes or clothes caught on branches. Nancy spotted a snake slithering into the hollow of a log, and mosquitoes bit her face and arms.

After about ten minutes, they reached a spit of land jutting into an isolated bayou. Birds chattered noisily as they flew for cover. A heron looked briefly toward the shore before continuing to fish among the cypress knobs at the water's edge. It was one of the most beautiful, and haunting, places Nancy had ever seen.

"Take a good look around, ladies," Mr. Legarde said. "Because this is the last sight you'll ever see."

Chapter
Twenty

F RANK CROUCHED down in the woods and gestured for Joe and Faye to do the same. "There they are, next to that bayou," he whispered.

Tailing Legarde's Jeep hadn't been easy. They'd had trouble getting a taxi, but it had taken Legarde a few minutes to pull away from the curb. When they finally hailed a taxi, Joe had instructed their driver to stay well behind the Jeep so that Mr. Legarde wouldn't spot them. The result was that they'd lost sight of the Jeep a few times. Frank was beginning to think they'd lost it altogether, when he happened to glance down a rutted road and saw the Jeep parked about a hundred yards down. They'd asked the taxi driver to pull around the next bend, out of sight of the rutted road. Then Frank, Faye, and Joe had come the rest of the way on foot, following the girls' muddy footprints through the woods.

"What's he doing now?" Faye whispered, her eyes focused on the group ahead.

Frank, Faye, and Joe were about fifty feet from the bayou, crouched behind a thick bush. Frank couldn't hear what Legarde or the girls were saying, but he saw the pistol Legarde kept pointed at them. He waved them toward the water, and, their hands bound, they began wading slowly in.

Frank saw the expression on Joe's face darken as he watched what was happening. Turning to Frank, Joe mouthed, "He's going to kill them!"

"Not if we can help it," Frank whispered back. Slowly, he crept forward, stepping from bush to bush. Luckily, Legarde had his back to them. If Frank could just get Nancy's attention, they might have a chance of overpowering Legarde.

She was holding back, he noticed, her eyes darting around. When she glanced in their direction, Frank took a chance and stuck his head out from behind the live oak he was using for cover.

Yes! Nancy's eyes rested on Frank for the briefest instant, but he was sure she'd seen him. He gave her the thumbs-up sign, then took a few more steps. . . .

Sna-ap!

Faye's foot landed in the middle of a dry branch, cracking it in half. She froze, but it was too late. Randall Legarde whirled around and pointed his gun in the direction of the sound.

"No!" Nancy cried. She lunged for the shore,

then lashed out with her left leg in a judo kick that sent Legarde's gun flying into the brush.

As Legarde scrambled after the weapon, Joe yelled, "Come on!"

Frank was already tearing through the brush toward the man. He was barely aware of branches whipping at his face and snagging his jeans. Just a few more yards, he thought.

Frank dived for the pistol a split second before Legarde. Out of the corner of his eye, he saw Joe hit Legarde in a flying tackle that sent both of them to the ground. Frank's hand closed around the pistol, and in a single motion he rolled onto his feet and stood up, pointing the pistol at Legarde.

"Give up, Mr. Legarde," he said. "It's over."

"Wow," Nancy said the next evening. "Remy's shrimp *remoulade* is fantastic!"

"So is the stuffed soft-shell crab," Bess said, grinning. "Almost being killed and dumped in a bayou sure does make a person appreciate the good things in life—like Remy's cooking!"

The two of them were sitting at the Royal Creole's best table, along with Shelley, Frank, Joe, Faye, and Mr. Gatlin. As Nancy looked around the table, she couldn't think of a better way to celebrate having solved their cases.

"I'm just glad all of you are safe," said Hugh Gatlin, smiling warmly at Faye. "And that my money's been recovered, of course."

"Me, too, Daddy," Faye said as she raised her glass in a toast. "Let's just think of this as a continuation of your birthday dinner that you and I had before all of this happened."

"It's the best present I could possibly get," Mr. Gatlin said as he clinked glasses with his daughter.

Half of the stolen money had been in the fan in Paul Dupre's carriage house. The police had found the rest in Randall Legarde's Jeep. When questioned about it, Legarde had admitted to taking the money from Mike's body after killing him.

"It's hard to believe," Mr. Gatlin added, shaking his head. "Randall Legarde and Bill Jacobson both in jail, as well as Paul Dupre. New Orleans will be reeling from the news for some time."

"I can't help feeling sorry for Danielle, though. After all, I've known her since she was a little girl."

Nancy hadn't particularly liked Danielle's attitude, but she knew the young singer must be having a hard time of it. "What's going to happen to her?" Nancy asked. "Will the club close?"

"She and J. J. are going to try to keep the club open," Mr. Gatlin said. "Danielle's got a good head for business, and she may be able to make it work. In the meantime, I've told her she can sing as many nights as she wants on the riverboat. The customers love her."

"I'm glad," Nancy said, and meant it.

"I hear they picked up Bill Jacobson at the *Morning Sun* and that he didn't try to resist arrest," Bess said.

"That's right," Mr. Gatlin said. "And according

to Detective Rollins, Jacobson has agreed to testify against Legarde in exchange for a lighter sentence."

"I guess the Royal Creole will have to make it without a rave review from Jacobson," Joe commented. "But judging by how packed this place is tonight, I don't think that'll be a problem."

"Definitely not," Shelley agreed. "Especially now that we know Remy *wasn't* being targeted by the competition."

Looking across the table, Frank asked, "What about that restaurant owner who was sneaking around here the night Remy opened the Royal Creole? What was *her* story?"

"We found out that she *was* trying to steal culinary secrets from Remy. When we were able finally to confront her about it, she confessed to stealing a couple of Remy's recipes.

"Bill Jacobson told the police that when Ms. Thibaud met him at Commander's Palace, she bragged about some new recipes," Shelley said. "Artichoke stuffed with shrimp and andouille sausage and crawfish *boudin*—"

"Which happen to be the same recipes Remy left near the back windows the afternoon we saw Ms. Thibaud sneaking around in the garden," Nancy said.

"She actually seemed proud about it," Bess put in.

"According to the cops, Jacobson had given Thibaud's Creole Kitchen a mediocre review a few years ago, and she was trying to convince him to give her another chance—using Remy's recipes to get a better review," Shelley added. "Jacobson always eats Sunday brunch at Commander's Palace, so she knew where to find him."

Nancy glanced at a passing couple, then did a double take when she realized the woman was Angela Dixon. She was wearing a scoop-necked emerald green dress that set off her red hair. With her was a good-looking man Nancy didn't recognize. Nancy saw the nervous look in Shelley's eyes as Angela stopped next to their table.

"I heard about Mr. Legarde," Angela said, frowning. "What a creep, huh?"

"Mmm," Shelley said, cautiously eyeing Angela.

Angela took a deep breath. "Look, I just wanted to say . . . well, finding out my boss is a crook has made me look at things differently," she said. "Life is short. I'm not about to waste it crying over the past."

Angela hadn't mentioned Remy by name, but Nancy was sure that she was referring to him.

"Unbelievable!" Bess whispered in Nancy's ear, as Angela and her date moved away. "I guess that means she'll be leaving Shelley and Remy alone from now on."

"I hope so," Nancy said.

Glancing across the table, she saw Frank and Faye leaning close together, laughing. She looked quickly away, feeling a slight pang of jealousy. But when her eyes wandered back to Frank, she saw he was smiling at her.

"I'd like to make a toast," he said. Getting to his feet, Frank raised his glass—and looked straight at Nancy. "To friends."

As Nancy smiled back, any awkwardness she'd felt faded away completely. "To friends," she agreed.

Now your younger brothers or sisters
can take a walk down Fear Street....

R•L•STINE'S
GHOSTS OF FEAR STREET ®

1	Hide and Shriek	52941-2/$3.99
2	Who's Been Sleeping in My Grave?	52942-0/$3.99
3	Attack of the Aqua Apes	52943-9/$3.99
4	Nightmare in 3-D	52944-7/$3.99
5	Stay Away From the Tree House	52945-5/$3.99
6	Eye of the Fortuneteller	52946-3/$3.99
7	Fright Knight	52947-1/$3.99
8	The Ooze	52948-X/$3.99
9	Revenge of the Shadow People	52949-8/$3.99
10	The Bugman Lives	52950-1/$3.99
11	The Boy Who Ate Fear Street	00183-3/$3.99
12	Night of the Werecat	00184-1/$3.99
13	How to be a Vampire	00185-X/$3.99
14	Body Switchers from Outer Space	00186-8/$3.99
15	Fright Christmas	00187-6/$3.99
16	Don't Ever get Sick at Granny's	00188-4/$3.99
17	House of a Thousand Screams	00190-6/$3.99
18	Camp Fear Ghouls	00191-4/$3.99

A MINSTREL BOOK

Christopher Pike presents....
a frighteningly fun new series for your younger brothers and sisters!

The Secret Path	53725-3/$3.50
The Howling Ghost	53726-1/$3.50
The Haunted Cave	53727-X/$3.50
Aliens in the Sky	53728-8/$3.99
The Cold People	55064-0/$3.99
The Witch's Revenge	55065-9/$3.99
The Dark Corner	55066-7/$3.99
The Little People	55067-5/$3.99
The Wishing Stone	55068-3/$3.99
The Wicked Cat	55069-1/$3.99
The Deadly Past	55072-1/$3.99
The Hidden Beast	55073-X/$3.99
The Creature in the Teacher	
	00261-9/$3.99
The Evil House	00262-7/$3.99
Invasion of the No-Ones	
	00263-5/$3.99

A MINSTREL® BOOK

THE HARDY BOYS CASEFILES™

☐ #1: DEAD ON TARGET	73992-1/$3.99		☐ #85: WINNER TAKE ALL	79469-8/$3.99
☐ #2: EVIL, INC.	73668-X/$3.99		☐ #86: VIRTUAL VILLAINY	79470-1/$3.99
☐ #3: CULT OF CRIME	68726-3/$3.99		☐ #87: DEAD MAN IN DEADWOOD	79471-X/$3.99
☐ #4: THE LAZARUS PLOT	73995-6/$3.75		☐ #88: INFERNO OF FEAR	79472-8/$3.99
☐ #8: SEE NO EVIL	73673-6/$3.50		☐ #89: DARKNESS FALLS	79473-6/$3.99
☐ #12: PERFECT GETAWAY	73675-2/$3.50		☐ #91: HOT WHEELS	79475-2/$3.99
☐ #14: TOO MANY TRAITORS	73677-9/$3.50		☐ #92: SABOTAGE AT SEA	79476-0/$3.99
☐ #32: BLOOD MONEY	74665-0/$3.50		☐ #93: MISSION: MAYHEM	88204-X/$3.99
☐ #35: THE DEAD SEASON	74105-5/$3.50		☐ #94: A TASTE FOR TERROR	88205-8/$3.99
☐ #41: HIGHWAY ROBBERY	70038-3/$3.75		☐ #95: ILLEGAL PROCEDURE	88206-6/$3.99
☐ #44: CASTLE FEAR	74615-4/$3.75		☐ #96: AGAINST ALL ODDS	88207-4/$3.99
☐ #45: IN SELF-DEFENSE	70042-1/$3.75		☐ #97: PURE EVIL	88208-2/$3.99
☐ #47: FLIGHT INTO DANGER	70044-8/$3.99		☐ #98: MURDER BY MAGIC	88209-0/$3.99
☐ #49: DIRTY DEEDS	70046-4/$3.99		☐ #99: FRAME-UP	88210-4/$3.99
☐ #50: POWER PLAY	70047-2/$3.99		☐ #100: TRUE THRILLER	88211-2/$3.99
☐ #53: WEB OF HORROR	73089-4/$3.99		☐ #101: PEAK OF DANGER	88212-0/$3.99
☐ #54: DEEP TROUBLE	73090-8/$3.99		☐ #102: WRONG SIDE OF THE LAW	88213-9/$3.99
☐ #56: HEIGHT OF DANGER	73092-4/$3.99		☐ #103: CAMPAIGN OF CRIME	88214-7/$3.99
☐ #57: TERROR ON TRACK	73093-2/$3.99		☐ #104: WILD WHEELS	88215-5/$3.99
☐ #60: DEADFALL	73096-7/$3.75		☐ #105: LAW OF THE JUNGLE	50428-2/$3.99
☐ #61: GRAVE DANGER	73097-5/$3.99		☐ #106: SHOCK JOCK	50429-0/$3.99
☐ #65: NO MERCY	73101-7/$3.99		☐ #107: FAST BREAK	50430-4/$3.99
☐ #66: THE PHOENIX EQUATION	73102-5/$3.99		☐ #108: BLOWN AWAY	50431-2/$3.99
☐ #69: MAYHEM IN MOTION	73105-X/$3.75		☐ #109: MOMENT OF TRUTH	50432-0/$3.99
☐ #72: SCREAMERS	73108-4/$3.75		☐ #110: BAD CHEMISTRY	50433-9/$3.99
☐ #73: BAD RAP	73109-2/$3.99		☐ #111: COMPETITIVE EDGE	50446-0/$3.99
☐ #75: NO WAY OUT	73111-4/$3.99		☐ #112: CLIFF-HANGER	50453-3/$3.99
☐ #76: TAGGED FOR TERROR	73112-2/$3.99		☐ #113: SKY HIGH	50454-1/$3.99
☐ #77: SURVIVAL RUN	79461-2/$3.99		☐ #114: CLEAN SWEEP	50456-8/$3.99
☐ #78: THE PACIFIC CONSPIRACY	79462-0/$3.99		☐ #115: CAVE TRAP	50462-2/$3.99
☐ #79: DANGER UNLIMITED	79463-9/$3.99		☐ #116: ACTING UP	50488-6/$3.99
☐ #80: DEAD OF NIGHT	79464-7/$3.99		☐ #117: BLOOD SPORT	56117-0/$3.99
☐ #81: SHEER TERROR	79465-5/$3.99		☐ #118: THE LAST LEAP	56118-9/$3.99
☐ #82: POISONED PARADISE	79466-3/$3.99		☐ #119: THE EMPEROR'S SHIELD	56119-7/$3.99
☐ #83: TOXIC REVENGE	79467-1/$3.99		☐ #120: SURVIVAL OF THE FITTEST	56120-0/$3.99
☐ #84: FALSE ALARM	79468-X/$3.99		☐ #121: ABSOLUTE ZERO	56121-9/$3.99